La semana de colores

THE WEEK
OF COLORS

ELENA GARRO

Translated from Spanish by

MEGAN MCDOWELL

TWO LINES
PRESS

Originally published in Spanish as *La semana de colores*

D. R. © 2021, Roberto Tabla, por la titularidad de los derechos patrimoniales.

D. R. © 2024, derechos de edición mundiales en lengua castellana: Penguin Random House Grupo Editorial, S. A. de C. V. Blvd. Miguel de Cervantes Saavedra núm. 301, 1er piso, colonia Granada, alcaldía Miguel Hidalgo, C. P. 11520, Ciudad de México.
Translation copyright © 2025 by Megan McDowell

Two Lines Press
www.twolinespress.com

ISBN: 978-1-949641-89-9
Ebook ISBN: 978-1-949641-90-5

Cover design by Vivian Lopez Rowe
Typeset by schubet

Library of Congress Cataloging-in-Publication Data
Names: Garro, Elena author | McDowell, Megan translator
Title: The week of colors / Elena Garro, Megan McDowell.
Other titles: Semana de colores. English
Description: San Francisco, CA : Two Lines Press, 2025. | "Originally published in Spanish as La semana de colores"--Title page verso.
Identifiers: LCCN 2025017522 (print) | LCCN 2025017523 (ebook) |
ISBN 9781949641899 paperback | ISBN 9781949641905 epub
Subjects: LCSH: Garro, Elena--Translations into English | LCGFT: Short stories
Classification: LCC PQ7297.G3585 S413 2025 (print) | LCC PQ7297. G3585 (ebook) | DDC 863/.64--dc23/eng/20250509
LC record available at https://lccn.loc.gov/2025017522
LC ebook record available at https://lccn.loc.gov/2025017523

Printed in the United States of America

1 3 5 7 9 10 8 6 4 2

TABLE OF CONTENTS

INTRODUCTION

The complexity of Elena Garro's convulsive life may be the reason why her public persona tends to receive more attention than her work. For example, she attended the Second International Congress of the Alliance of Antifascist Writers for the Defense of Culture during the Spanish Civil War. She had just turned 21 and while there she likely had lunch with André Malraux and Robert Capa, or sheltered during a shelling with Pablo Neruda or Langston Hughes. There are very few pictures of her from that period. Still, in a very well-known one, she is walking on La Rambla of Barcelona on the arm of Octavio Paz, then her husband, also absurdly good-looking at 23.

This was in 1937 and by then she had already left her theatre studies at the National Autonomous University of Mexico, where she had been admitted in the surprisingly early year of 1934—even though higher education was gender integrated in the nineteenth century in Mexico, it was uncommon for women to attend until the second half of the twentieth century.

After the birth of Helena Paz in 1939, Garro wrote journalism, plays, and film scripts. She published a series of articles about influential women in Mexico—she may have been the first writer who perceived the importance of Frida Kahlo as an artist all by her own right, and not as the wife of Diego Rivera. At least one of her early scripts, *Las señoritas Vivanco*—written with Juan de la Cabada and Josefina Vicens—is considered a classic. In that period, in which she was following Octavio Paz through his diplomatic destinies, she developed a professional relationship with José Bianco, the editor of *Sur*, the Argentinian magazine directed by Victoria Ocampo. It was through Bianco that she met—in Paris, where Paz was the second secretary of the Mexican Embassy—Adolfo Bioy Casares, with whom she sustained a 20-year, mainly epistolary love affair. Bioy Casares was a novelist and part of the very core of the *Sur* group. He was married to the poet and fiction writer Silvina Ocampo—sister of Victoria—and was Jorge Luis Borges's best friend; they famously had lunch together every day. This intellectual group offered Garro a remote, but not insignificant, window into a literary life, and, maybe more importantly, a breathing space outside the power sphere of Octavio Paz, whom she finally separated from in 1959.

Her first novel, *Recollections of Things to Come*, was rejected in 1962 by the legendary Spanish publisher Carlos

Barral because he believed that there were no readers for what was then beginning to be called "magical realism." The book was then published with tremendous success by Joaquín Mortiz in Mexico and won the 1963 Xavier Villaurrutia Prize.

Much has been said about the influence of *Recollections of Things to Come* on Gabriel García Márquez's *One Hundred Years of Solitude*, published four years later, in 1967. Both books share a familial air and were innovative for similar reasons, but neither he nor she ever acknowledged any influence from the other. They were friends, though, and even if we will never know if they read each other, they surely enjoyed dancing together. There are some famous pictures of Garro and García Márquez dancing the twist, and during the political nightmare she found herself in a few years later, she told a CIA informant that Lee Harvey Oswald used to attend those "twist parties."

Recollections of Things to Come was a novel that showed Elena Garro's sympathy for what was called during most of the twentieth century the Agrarian Movement—a loose coalition of organizations and political leaders identified with what was left of the peasant armies of Emiliano Zapata after the Revolution of 1910. Maybe because of the socialist nature of that coalition, in 1968 Garro was randomly accused in a newspaper article of being an instigator of the vigorous student uprising that was threatening the Olympic Games. She reacted not only by denying the charges but also denouncing leftist intellectuals and their conspiracies in a magazine article; she also wrote letters with lists of names to politicians. This forced her to live like an exile for a quarter of a century, first hiding in hostels and pensions in Mexico City—she sincerely thought that she was going to be killed by communists—and then in New York, Madrid, and Paris. It was at the beginning of this crisis that her affair with Adolfo Bioy Casares came to an end. Imagining that she would be on the run for a long time, she sent to Buenos Aires a box with her four cats. Silvina Ocampo, Bioy's wife, was a dog person, so the cats were sent to the country house, which broke Garro's heart.

For years, depending on whom and where you asked about Elena Garro in Mexico, the answer would be that she was a traitor to the left or a leftist betrayed by the right; a friend of brutal oppressors or a brutally oppressed woman. Now it's clear that both positions were historically accurate: life is long, and she was a writer, not a nun.

Time—and the accumulation of critical works that are less and less ideologically based—has settled the dust of those discussions. Now, if Mexican literature were divided by Garro's figure, it would be between those who belong to the church of her writing and those who don't—and the second group must not be trusted. Garro had an original voice whose influence still reverberates in active, brilliant writers like Carmen Boullosa or Luis Felipe Fabre; she was the author of aphoristic visions that stay revolving forever in her readers' minds; here are some pieces of that epigrammatic wisdom in Megan McDowell's translation of *The Week of Colors*:

> "It was a day with two days inside it."
> "–Are you sure the other world is as nice
> as this one? –Yes, and since we don't have
> a body, we don't sweat."
> "The street is the street and what belongs
> to the street belongs to us all."

She was a bold innovator with an extraordinary ear for the syntax and lexicon of marginal voices: working-class women, Mexicans for whom Spanish is a second language, children. And she was a master of transparency: no matter how weird and experimental the story she was telling, it's always clear, concrete, and meaningful.

In Elena Garro's formative years as a writer, prose, to be prestigious, needed a specific sonority and an academic diction: Alfonso Reyes, Jorge Luis Borges, José Ortega y Gasset, Teresa de la Parra—most but not all of them men— or, of course, Octavio Paz, were all authors whose aspiration to a sculptural style was so strong that many times it's distinguishable without attribution. Garro, who suffered the unbearable weight of finding her own literary voice surrounded by those oppressive figures, made a statement out of writing in a tone that did not search for monumentality but its opposite: an organic flair that produced a sensation of naturality, a language so very studied it felt minimally manipulated.

The stories in *The Week of Colors* use point of view as a tool to expose what is painful or uncomfortable for those stripped of power. There is a clear identification of women, indigenous servants, and children as people whose agency has been taken away, but as in everything with Garro, things are not obvious or schematic: in "Mercury," the character who can't control his destiny is a rich young man whose aspiration to happiness is undermined by a very convenient marriage; in "Perfecto Luna" it's a skeleton who successfully claims the right to express himself.

In the magisterial "It's the Tlaxcaltecas' Fault," the continuity of actions and presences between a couple in modern Mexico City and Tenochtitlan in 1521 happens as if the writer were just a notary documenting the impossible. In the comings and goings between times and landscapes, a meditation on memory as the gravitational center of all moral actions is slowly constructed, while more common, political questions come to the surface of the story: about a woman's position in the modern world, about the perpetuation of colonial exploitation after the War of Independence and the Revolution of 1910, about the infliction of pain as the unique strategy of the hegemonic powers to keep their position. The rules of magical realism apply to the story, but its ultimate result is a deep existential meditation: Laura and Nacha remember who they are, so they are whole, free people, even if they are subjects of oppression—one for being a wife, the other for being a servant. Pablo, the abusive husband and house master, is a slave with an illusion of power because his lack of memory makes him foreign to his humanity; he is an empty vessel occupied only by anger.

In "The Tree," the cycle of revolutionary violence is actualized in a parodic key within the microcosmos of a petit bourgeois home. The criollo lady who owns the house does not understand how aggravating for her servants her mere existence is. And the servant who confronts her will not find her place in modern Mexico even if she mounts a successful, empty rebellion. Revolutions, Garro seems to have thought, are about ideas, not about replacing one master for another.

There is nothing simple or accidental in the only apparently candid stories of Elena Garro. In "The Gnome," Eva and Leli spend the slow summer mornings of the country house lying in a beautiful tropical garden, languidly speaking about death. Eva, a curious soul, takes the initiative of eating a forbidden fruit and sharing it with her sister, just to see what happens after death—anything is better, after all, than paradisiacal boredom. None in the family understands Eva's research interest in the next life, except her younger sister, Estrella, who looks at everything from the top of the house: the eye of God in a world in which only innocence can be considered divine, even when the borderline between childhood candor and monstrosity is hard to draw. Finding unknown worlds, little Eva seems to think, involves taking risks, especially when the speaker is in the outer ring of power.

⌛

There is a sonnet by the baroque Mexican poet Sor Juana Inés de la Cruz that Elena Garro must have known well. The poem can be read as a secular prayer for indomitable women breaking through the well-defended walls of male-dominated literary circles. In the first two quartets of the sonnet, Sor Juana presents the problem by listing situations that demanded extreme bravery of men: weathering a storm in the open ocean, bullfighting, taming a wild horse. In the concluding tercets of the poem, she says that all of that requires real courage, but, in Edith Grossman's translation:

> If there were someone valiant enough
> That, despite the danger, he would attempt
> To drive with daring hand the swift chariot
> Bathed in the light of great Apollo himself
> He might do all this, but never enter
> A state that must last the rest of his life.

For her, to be a poet—that is, to be Apollo's child—one could not serve another master than poetry—and she was a nun who had supposedly chosen to be a wife of Christ.

The rebellious Sor Juana was silenced in her early for-
ties and died a couple of years later, at 44, serving as a con-
vent nurse during a plague in 1695. The pious critics of past
centuries used to say that she found, late in her life, her true
vocation as God's servant. No one thinks that today: the
Church had taken poetry from her, so she had no interest
in staying alive.

Elena Garro learned Sor Juana's lesson and achieved
what the poet could not, no matter the multitude of storms
she endured: she kept writing and publishing until her very
last breath, when she was 81 years old. The publication of
Elena Garro's first collection, well into the twenty-first
century and impeccably translated into English by Megan
McDowell, offers the opportunity of reading her as I think
she would have liked to be read: as the damned good writer
that she was.

Álvaro Enrigue

IT'S THE TLAXCALTECAS' FAULT

Nacha heard a knock at the kitchen door and froze. When the knock came again, she crept steathily over to open the door and peered out into the night. Señora Laura emerged from the darkness with a finger over her lips. She was still wearing the white dress, burned and smeared with dirt and blood.

"Ma'am!" sighed Nacha.

Señora Laura tiptoed in and looked at the cook with questioning eyes. Then, reassured, she sat down beside the stove and surveyed her kitchen as if she'd never seen it before.

"Nachita, give me a cup of coffee... I'm cold."

"Ma'am, the master...the master is going to kill you. We'd already given you up for dead."

"Dead?"

Laura gazed in amazement at the kitchen's white tiles, then put her feet up on the chair and wrapped her arms around her knees in a thoughtful pose. Nacha put water on to boil for the coffee and looked at her mistress out of the corner of her eye; she couldn't think of a single word to say. The lady rested her head on her knees and seemed very sad.

"You know what, Nacha? It's the Tlaxcaltecas' fault."

Nacha didn't answer, looking instead at the water that wasn't boiling.

Outside, night blurred the garden's roses and shadowed the fig trees. Far beyond their branches, lighted windows gleamed in the neighboring houses. The kitchen was separated from the world by an invisible wall of sadness, a caesura.

"You don't agree, Nacha?"

"Yes, ma'am…"

"I'm like them: a traitor…" said Laura dolefully.

The cook crossed her arms, waiting for the water to start bubbling.

"And you, Nacha, are you a traitor?"

She looked hopeful. If Nacha shared her traitorous nature, she would understand, and Laura needed someone to understand her that night.

Nacha reflected for a few seconds, turned toward the water that was coming to a rattling boil, and poured it over the coffee. The warm aroma made her feel at ease with her mistress.

"Yes, I am a traitor too, Señora Laurita."

Feeling pleased, Nacha poured the coffee into a white cup, added two sugar cubes, and set it on the table in front of the lady. Laura, lost in thought, took a few sips.

"You know what, Nachita? Now I know why we had so many accidents on that damned trip to Guanajuato. We ran out of gas in Mil Cumbres. Margarita got scared because it was getting dark. A trucker gave us a little fuel so we could make it to Morelia. Then, in Cuitzeo, when we were crossing the white bridge, the car stopped all of a sudden. Margarita got huffy with me—you know how she's afraid of empty roads and Indians' eyes. When a car full of tourists came by, she went with them to town to find a mechanic and I stayed in the middle of the white bridge, which crosses the dry lake with the white stone bottom. The light was very white, and the bridge, the stone, and the car started to float in it. Then the light broke into pieces, turning into thousands of tiny spinning dots, until it became fixed like a portrait. Time had been completely turned over, like when you look at a postcard and then flip it to see what's written on the back. That's how I arrived at Lake Cuitzeo, and at the other child I once was. Light brings on those catastrophes, when the sun turns white and you're in the very center of its rays. Thoughts also turn into a thousand dots and their spinning can make you dizzy. I looked at the fabric of my white dress, and that's when I heard his footsteps. I was not surprised. I raised my eyes and saw him coming. Just then I remembered the magnitude of my betrayal; I was afraid and wanted to run away. But time closed in around me, it turned singular and perishable, and I couldn't move from the seat of the car. Someday you will find yourself facing your own actions turned into immutable stones, just like that stone there, I was told as a child when I was shown the image of a god—I don't remember now which one. We forget everything, don't we, Nachita? But it's only forgotten for a while. Back then, words also seemed to be made of stone, but of a fluid and crystalline kind. The stone solidified as each word ended, to be written forever in time. Weren't the words of your elders like that?"

Nacha reflected for a few seconds, then nodded with certainty.

"Yes they were, Señora Laurita."

"The terrible thing, which I discovered in that instant, is that everything incredible is true. There he was coming toward me along the side of the bridge, his skin sunburned and his shoulders burdened with defeat. His footsteps sounded like dry leaves. His eyes were shining. Their black sparks reached me from far away, and I saw his black hair streaming in the very white light of that encounter. Before I could get away from him, he was there before my eyes. He stopped, grabbed hold of the car door, and looked at me. He had a cut on his left hand, his hair was full of dust, and the blood flowing from a wound on his shoulder was so red it seemed black. He didn't say anything, but I knew he was fleeing in defeat. He wanted to tell me that I deserved death, telling me at the same time that my death would bring about his. He was gravely injured, and he was looking for me.

"It's the Tlaxcaltecas' fault, I told him. He looked up toward the sky. Then his eyes settled on mine once again.

"What are you up to? he asked me in his deep voice. I couldn't tell him I had gotten married, because I am married to him. There are some things you just can't say, you know that, Nachita.

"What about the others? I asked him.

"The ones who got out alive are in the same plight as me, he said. I saw that each word pained his tongue, and I fell silent, thinking of the shame of my betrayal.

"Then I said, You know I'm afraid, and that's why I am a traitor…

"I know, he replied, and lowered his head. He's known me since I was little, Nacha. His father and mine were brothers, and we were cousins. He always loved me, or at least so he said, and so we all believed. I was ashamed there on the bridge. The blood kept flowing over his chest. I took a handkerchief from my pocket and without a word I started to wipe it away. I always loved him too, Nachita, because he is my opposite: he is unafraid, and no traitor. He took my hand and looked at it.

"It's very discolored. It looks like one of their hands, he said.

"It's been a long time since the sun shone on me, I explained. He lowered his head and dropped my hand. We stood like that, in silence, hearing the blood flow over his chest. He didn't reproach me for anything; he knows well what I'm capable of. But on his chest the trickling blood wrote that his heart still held my words and my body. Then I knew, Nachita, that time and love are a single thing.

"And my house? I asked him.

"Let's go see it. He took hold of me with his hot hand, the way he used to take hold of his shield, and I realized he wasn't carrying it. He lost it when he fled, I thought, and I let him lead me. In the Cuitzeo light, his steps sounded same as in the other light: muffled and mild. We walked

7

through the city that burned on the water's shores. I closed my eyes. I already told you, Nacha, that I'm a coward. Or maybe it was the smoke and dust that drew my tears. I sat down on a rock and covered my face with my hands: I can't walk anymore…

"We're here, he replied. He knelt down beside me and caressed my white dress with his fingertips.

"If you don't want to see how it turned out, don't look, he whispered.

"His black hair lent me shade. He wasn't angry, only sad. Before, I never would have dared to kiss him, but now I have learned not to have respect for man, and I embraced his neck and kissed him on the mouth.

"You have always been in the loveliest room of my heart, he told me. He lowered his head and looked at the earth strewn with dry stones. He used one of them to draw two parallel lines, which he lengthened out until they joined together and became one.

"They are you and me, he said without looking up. Nachita, I was left speechless.

"It won't be long now until time ends and we become one…that's why I was looking for you, he said. Nacha, I had forgotten that when time runs out, the two of us must end up one in the other, to enter true time as one. When he said that, I looked him in the eyes. Before, I had only dared to meet his eyes when he took me, but now, as I told you, I've learned not to respect a man's eyes. It's also true that I didn't want to see what was happening around me… I'm very cowardly. I remembered the battle cries and I heard them again:

8

strident, burning in the middle of morning. I also heard the stones striking and saw them go whizzing over my head. He moved to kneel in front of me and crossed his arms over my head to make a shelter.

"This is the end of man, I said.

"That's true, he replied, his voice over mine. And I saw myself in his eyes and in his body. Would it be a deer that brought me to his hillside? Or a star that launched me up to write signals in the sky? His voice wrote signs in blood on my chest and my white dress was left striped like a red and white tiger.

"I'll come back at night, wait for me… he sighed. He picked up his shield and looked at me from high above.

"It won't be long until we're one, he added, with the same courtesy as always.

"When he left, I heard the shouts of combat again. I took off running under the rain of rocks and got lost, and there was the car stopped on the bridge of Cuitzeo Lake.

"What happened? Are you hurt? Margarita cried out when she came back. Frightened, she touched the blood on my white dress and pointed to the blood on my lips and the dirt caked in my hair. From the other car, the mechanic from Cuitzeo looked at me with his dead eyes.

"These wild Indians…! You can't leave a lady alone! he said as he leapt from his car, supposedly to come to my aid.

"We reached Mexico City when it got dark. How it had changed, Nachita, I almost can't believe it! At twelve noon the warriors had still been there, and now there was no trace of their existence. Nor was there rubble left behind.

We went past the sad, silent Zócalo; of the other plaza—nothing was left! Margarita looked at me out of the corner of her eyes. When we reached the house, you opened up for us. Remember?"

Nacha nodded. It was true that only two short months ago Señora Laurita and her mother-in-law Margarita had taken a trip to Guanajuato. The night they'd returned, Josefina the maid and she, Nacha, had noticed the lady's vacant eyes and the blood on her dress, but Señora Margarita had signaled to them not to say anything. She had seemed very concerned. Later on, Josefina told her that at the table, the master had stared crossly at his wife and said, "Why didn't you change? Do you *like* to remember the bad things?"

Señora Margarita, his mother, had already told him what had happened, and she motioned to him as though saying, "Quiet, have pity on her!" Señora Laurita didn't answer; she caressed her mouth and smiled slyly. Then the master went back to talking about President López Mateos.

"You know that name is forever on his lips," Josefina had scoffed.

Deep down, they thought Señora Laurita must get bored at having to always hear about the president and his official visits.

"Just imagine, Nachita, I had never noticed how bored I got with Pablo until that night!" the lady said, lovingly hugging her knees and proving Josefina and Nacha right.

The cook crossed her arms and nodded.

"After I came back to the house, I found that furniture, the vases, and the mirrors loomed over me and left me sadder than I had been before. How many days, how many years will I have to go on waiting until my cousin comes for me? That's what I thought about, and I regretted my betrayal. At dinner I noticed how Pablo didn't speak in words, but in letters. And I started to count them while I looked at his fat mouth and his one dead eye. Suddenly, he went quiet. You know how he forgets everything. He sat there with his arms at his sides: this new husband has no memory, and he knows nothing beyond the everyday things.

"You have a gloomy and confused husband, he said to me, turning to look at the stains on my dress. My poor mother-in-law was shaken, and since we were already having coffee, she got up to put on a twist.

"To cheer you up, she told us, forcing a smile, because she could see the argument coming.

"We sat there in silence. The house filled up with noise. I looked at Pablo. He looks like... and I didn't dare say the name out of fear that they could read my thoughts. It's true that he looks like him, Nacha. They both like the water and cool houses. They both gaze at the sky in the evenings, and both have black hair and white teeth. But Pablo speaks jumpily, gets angry over nothing, and constantly asks: What are you thinking about? My husband-cousin doesn't do or say any of that."

"Very true! It's true that the master is a nag!" Nacha said disdainfully.

Laura sighed and looked at her cook in relief. Thank goodness she had Nacha as a confidante.

"At night, as Pablo was kissing me, I repeated to myself:

What hour will he come for me? And I nearly cried remembering the blood from the wound on his shoulder. Nor could I forget his arms crossed to make a protective shelter over my head. At the same time, I was afraid Pablo would notice that my cousin had kissed me that morning. But he didn't notice anything, and if it hadn't been for Josefina scaring me the next morning, Pablo never would have known a thing."

Nachita agreed that Josefina with her taste for scandal was to blame for everything. She, Nacha, had told her: "Shut up! Shut up for the love of God—if they didn't hear our cries there's a reason for it!" But it was hopeless: no sooner did Josefina enter the master's bedroom with the breakfast tray than she blurted out what she should have kept to herself.

"Ma'am, last night a man was looking into your bedroom window! Nacha and I screamed and cried!"

"We didn't hear a thing..." said the master in surprise.

"It's him!" the mistress cried foolishly.

"Who is *him*?" asked the master, looking at his wife as if he were going to kill her. At least, that's what Josefina said later.

Señora Laurita was terrified and put a hand over her mouth, and when the master repeated his question, more angrily every time, she replied, "The Indian...the Indian who followed me from Cuitzeo to Mexico City..."

That's how Josefina found out about the Indian, and that's how she told Nachita about him.

"We must call the police immediately!" cried the master.

Josefina showed him the window the stranger had been peering into, and Pablo examined it carefully: there were bloody fingerprints on the sill, nearly fresh.

"He is wounded…" said Master Pablo, distressed. He took a few steps around the bedroom and stopped in front of his wife.

"He *was* an Indian, sir," said Josefina, corroborating Laura's words. Pablo saw the white dress tossed on a chair, and he grabbed it roughly.

"Can you explain where these stains came from?"

Señora Laurita was speechless as she stared at the blood-stains on the chest of her dress, and the master pounded his fist on the dresser. Then he went over to his wife and smacked her hard. Josefina saw it and heard it.

"His gestures are ferocious and his actions just as inco-herent as his words. It's not my fault he accepted his defeat," said Laura with contempt.

"Very true," agreed Nacha.

There was a long silence in the kitchen. Laura ran her fingertip along the bottom of her mug to scrape out the black coffee grounds that had gotten stuck there, and when Nacha saw her do that, she poured some more hot coffee.

"Drink your coffee, ma'am," she said, sympathizing with her mistress's heartache. After all, what was the master complaining about? Anyone could see from miles away that Señora Laurita was not for him.

"I fell in love with Pablo on a road, at a moment when he reminded me of someone I once knew, someone I didn't remember. Later, I sometimes recovered that moment, when it seemed like he was going to turn into that other man he resembled. But it wasn't true. Immediately, he once again became absurd, memory-less, and he only repeated the gestures of all the men in Mexico City. How could I not have realized the deception? When he gets angry, he forbids me from going out. You've seen it! How often has he made a scene in restaurants or at the movies? You know, Nachita. My cousin-husband, on the other hand, never, I mean never, gets angry at his wife."

Nacha knew the truth of what the lady was saying, and that was why, on that morning when Josefina had come into the kitchen frightened and shouting, "Wake Señora Margarita, the master is beating the mistress!" she, Nacha, had run to the older lady's room.

Master Pablo had been calmed by his mother's presence. Margarita was astonished to hear about the Indian, because she hadn't seen him at Cuitzeo Lake, she had only seen the blood, the same blood all of us could see.

"Maybe you got sunstroke at the lake, Laura, and you had a nosebleed. You see, son, we had the top down on the car," Margarita said, almost at a loss for words.

Señora Laura lay face down on the bed, lost in her thoughts, while her husband and mother-in-law argued.

"You know, Nachita, what I was thinking that morning? I thought: What if he saw me the night before when Pablo was kissing me? And I felt like crying. Then I remembered that when a man and a woman love each other and don't have children, they are doomed to become one. That's what my other father told me, when I brought him water and he looked at the door behind which my cousin-husband and I slept. Everything my other father had said to me was now coming true. Lying on the pillow, I heard Pablo and

Margarita's words, and they were nothing but nonsense. I'm going to find him, I thought to myself. But where? Later, when you came back to my room to ask what we should do for lunch, a thought came into my head: To the Café de Tacuba! And I had never even been to that cafe, Nachita, I'd only heard it talked about."

Nacha remembered as if she were watching it now: the mistress put on her white, bloodstained dress, the same one she was wearing right now in the kitchen.

"For God's sake, Laura, don't wear *that* dress!" her mother-in-law said. But Señora Laura didn't listen. She put a white sweater over it to hide the stains, buttoned it up to the neck, and left the house without saying goodbye. Then came the worst. No, not the worst. The worst was going to come now, in the kitchen, if Señora Margarita woke up.

"There was nobody at the Café de Tacuba. That place is very sad, Nachita. A waiter came over to me. What can I get you? I didn't want anything, but I had to order something. A coconut sweet. My cousin and I used to eat coconuts when we were little... There was a clock in the cafe that ticked away the time. In all cities there are clocks ticking time, and it must be gradually wearing away. When there's nothing left but a transparent layer, he will come for me and the two drawn lines will become one, and I will live in the loveliest room of his heart. That's what I told myself as I ate the sweet.

"What time is it? I asked the waiter.

"Twelve o'clock, miss.

"Pablo comes home at one, I thought. If I get a taxi

15

driver to take me by the ring road, I can still wait a while longer. But I didn't wait; I went out to the street. The sun was silvery, my thoughts became a shining dust, and there was no present, past, or future. My cousin was on the sidewalk, and he came to stand before me; his eyes were sad, and he looked at me for a long time.

"What are you doing? he asked in his deep voice.

"I was waiting for you.

"He went still as a panther. I saw his black hair and the red wound on his shoulder.

"Weren't you afraid of being here all alone? The rocks and the screams again flew around us, and I felt something burning behind me.

"Don't look, he told me. He put one knee on the ground and used his fingers to snuff out my dress, which had caught fire. I saw anguish in his eyes.

"Get me out of here! I screamed as loud as I could, because I remembered that I was in front of my father's house, that the house was burning, and that behind me were my parents and siblings, all dead. I saw it all in his eyes while he knelt there on the ground, putting out the flames on my dress. I fell on top of him, and he caught me in his arms. He covered my eyes with his hot hand.

"This is the end of man, I told him, my eyes under his hand.

"Don't watch!

"He pressed me to his heart. I heard it beat the way thunder rolls over the mountains. How long until time ended and I could hear it beat forever? My tears cooled his hand that burned in the city's flames. War cries and stones surrounded us, but I was safe beneath his chest.

"Sleep with me... he said in a very low voice.

"Did you see me last night? I asked him.

"I saw you...

"We slept in the morning light, in the heat of the flames. When we remembered, he rose and took up his shield.

"Hide until dawn. I will come for you.

"He dashed away on his bare legs... And I fled again, Nachita, because I was afraid to be alone.

"Miss, do you feel ok?

"A voice just like Pablo's reached me in the middle of the street.

"Villain! Leave me in peace!

"I hailed a taxi that brought me home on the ring road and I arrived..."

Nacha remembered Señora Laurita's arrival: she had opened the door herself, and she was the one to give her mistress the news. Josefina came afterward, practically tumbling down the stairs.

"Ma'am, the master and Señora Margarita are at the police station!"

Laura gaped at her, speechless.

"Where were you, ma'am?"

"I went to the Café de Tacuba."

"But that was two days ago."

Josefina was holding the newspaper *Últimas Noticias*. She read aloud: "Señora Aldama is still missing. It is believed that the sinister individual of indigenous appearance who followed her from Cuitzeo is a sadist. Police are investigating in the states of Michoacán and Guanajuato."

Señora Laurita snatched the paper out of Josefina's hands and tore it up, enraged. Then she went to her room. Nacha and Josefina followed her; it was best not to leave her alone. They watched her lie down on the bed and start dreaming with her eyes wide open. They both had the same thought, and they said it aloud later in the kitchen: "If you ask me, Señora Laurita is in love." When the master arrived, they were still in their mistress's room.

"Laura!" he cried. He rushed to the bed and took his wife in his arms.

"Soul of my soul!" he sobbed.

Señora Laurita seemed to soften for a few seconds.

"Sir!" cried Josefina. "The lady's dress is quite singed."

Nacha shot her a reproachful look. The master examined the lady's dress and legs.

"It's true...the soles of her shoes are burned, too. My love, what happened? Where were you?"

"At the Café de Tacuba," the mistress replied serenely.

Señora Margarita wrung her hands and moved closer to her daughter-in-law.

"We know that you were there the day before yesterday and that you ate a coconut sweet. What happened next?"

"I got a taxi and came here by the ring road."

Nacha lowered her eyes, Josefina opened her mouth as though to say something, and Señora Margarita bit her lip. Pablo, on the other hand, grabbed his wife by the shoulders and shook her hard.

"Stop acting like an idiot! Where were you for the past two days? Why is your dress burned?"

"Burned? But he put it out…" Señora Laura blurted.

"He…? That disgusting Indian?" Pablo shook her again with rage.

"I met him as I was coming out of the Café de Tacuba…" sobbed the lady, deathly afraid.

"I never thought you were so low!" growled the master, and he threw her onto the bed.

"Tell us who he is," pleaded Margarita, her voice softening.

"But I couldn't tell them he was my husband, could I, Nachita?" asked Laura, seeking the cook's approval.

Nacha applauded her mistress's discretion and remembered how on that day she had felt pity for Señora Laurita's situation and had offered, "Maybe the Cuitzeo Indian is a sorcerer."

"A sorcerer! You mean a murderer!"

After that, Señora Laurita wasn't allowed to leave her room for many days. The master ordered the house's doors and windows watched at all times. They, the two maids, went into the mistress's room constantly to check on her. Nacha always refused to give her opinion on the case, or to mention any anomalies that surprised her. But who could keep Josefina quiet?

"Sir, at dawn, the Indian was at the window again," she announced when she brought in the breakfast tray.

The master rushed to the window and again found the mark of fresh blood. The mistress started to cry.

"Poor thing…! Poor thing…!" she said between sobs.

That was the day the master brought in a doctor. After that, the doctor returned every day at dusk.

"He asked me about my childhood, about my father and mother. But Nachita, I didn't know which childhood, or which father or mother he wanted to know about. That's why I talked to him about the conquest of Mexico. You understand me, right?" Laura asked, her eyes on the yellow saucepans.

"Yes, ma'am…" And Nachita nervously peered out the window at the garden. The night revealed little among its shadows. She remembered the master's listless face at dinner, and his mother's look of mourning.

"Mother, Laura asked the doctor for *The Conquest of New Spain* by Bernal Díaz del Castillo. She says it's the only thing that interests her."

Señora Margarita dropped her fork.

"My poor son, your wife is insane!"

"She speaks of nothing but the fall of Great Tenochtitlán," added Master Pablo with a somber air.

Two days later, the doctor, Señora Margarita, and Master Pablo decided that Laura's depression was only worsening from being locked up. She needed to make contact with the world and face her responsibilities. Starting then, the master sent his wife out daily in the car to take short walks through Chapultepec Park. The lady went out in the company of her mother-in-law, and the driver had orders to keep a close watch on them. But the eucalyptus air did not improve her, for as soon as she returned home,

Señora Laurita went into her room to read *The Conquest of New Spain* by Bernal Díaz del Castillo.

One morning, Señora Margarita came back from Chapultepec Park alone and disconsolate.

"The madwoman has escaped!" she cried in a strident voice upon entering the house.

"You see, Nacha, I sat down on the same bench as always, and I said to myself, He will not forgive me. A man can forgive one, two, three, four betrayals, but not constant betrayal. This thought made me very sad. It was hot, and Margarita bought a vanilla ice cream; I didn't want one, so she got into the car to eat it. I realized that she was just as bored of me as I was of her. I don't like to be watched, and I tried to look at other things so as not to see her eating the ice cream cone and watching me. I saw gray moss hanging from the Montezuma cypresses, and, I don't know why, the morning turned as sad as those trees. They have seen the same catastrophes I have, I thought to myself. Along the empty sidewalk, the lonely hours passed. I was like those hours: alone on an empty sidewalk. My husband had seen my constant betrayal through the window, and he had abandoned me on that path made of nonexistent things. I remembered the smell of corn husks and the soft sound of his steps. That's how he used to walk, with the tempo of dry leaves as the February wind blew them over the stones. Back then, I didn't need to turn my head to know he was there, looking at my back... I was deep in those sad thoughts when I heard the sun move and the dry leaves start to change places. His breathing came closer to my back, and then he stood before me; I saw his bare feet in front of mine. He had a scratch on his knee. I raised my eyes and found myself under his. We went a long time without speaking. Out of respect, I waited for his words.

"What have you been up to? he asked.

"I saw that he didn't move and seemed sadder than before.

"I was waiting for you, I replied.

"The final day is almost here... It seemed like his voice came from the depths of time. His shoulder was still bleeding. I was filled with shame, and I looked down, opened my bag, and took out a handkerchief to wipe his chest. Then I put it away again. He stood still, observing me.

"Let's head to the Tacuba exit... There are many betrayals... he said.

"He took my hand, and we walked among people who screamed and moaned. There were many dead bodies floating in the canals. Women were sitting in the grass and watching them float by. Pestilence emanated from all sides, and the children cried as they ran from place to place, separated from their parents. I looked at it all without wanting to see it. The wrecked canoes carried no one, and only inspired sadness. My husband sat me down under a splintered tree. He put one knee on the ground and looked keenly at what was happening around us. He was not afraid. Then he looked at me.

"I know you are a traitor and bear good will toward me. Good grows alongside evil.

"I could hardly hear him over the children's cries. They

came from far away but were so loud they broke the day-light. It seemed like the last time they would cry.

"It's the children... he said.

"This is the end of man, I said again, because I could think of nothing else to say.

"He put his hands over my ears and then pressed me to his chest.

"You were a traitor when I met you and I loved you that way.

"You were born without luck, I told him, and I embraced him. My cousin-husband closed his eyes to keep his tears from escaping. We lay on the broken branches of the pepper tree. There we were pelted by the warriors' cries, by stones and the sobs of the children.

"Time is running out... my husband whispered.

"The women who didn't want to die with the day were fleeing through a crack. The ranks of men fell one after another, in a chain, as if they were holding hands and the same blow knocked them all over. Some gave such a loud battle cry that it kept echoing long after their death.

"There wasn't much time left before we became one forever, when my cousin got up, gathered some branches together, and made me a little shelter.

"Wait for me here.

"He looked at me and went off to fight, hoping to avoid defeat. I stayed huddled where I was. I didn't want to see the people fleeing, so as not to be tempted, or to see the bodies floating in the water, so as not to cry. I started to count the little berries that hung from the cut branches:

they were dry, and when I touched them their red shells fell off. I don't know why, but it seemed like a bad omen, and I looked instead at the sky, which was starting to darken. First it turned brown, then it began to take on the color of the drowned bodies in the canals. It made me recall the colors of other afternoons. But the evening went on turning black and blue, swelling up as if it were going to explode, and I knew that time had run out. What would become of me if my cousin didn't return? Perhaps he had already died in battle. I no longer cared about his fate, and I ran out of there as fast as I could, fear close at my heels. When he comes to look for me… I didn't have time to finish my thought because I found myself in the dusk of Mexico City. Margarita must have finished her vanilla ice cream, and Pablo must be very angry… A taxi brought me here by the ring road. And you know what, Nachita? The ring roads were the canals infested with cadavers…that's why I was so sad when I arrived… Now, Nachita, don't tell the master that I spent the afternoon with my husband."

Nachita settled her arms over her lilac skirt.

"Master Pablo left for Acapulco ten days ago. He got very skinny over the weeks of the investigation," Nacha explained, satisfied.

Laura looked at her without surprise and sighed in relief.

"It's Señora Margarita who's upstairs," Nacha added, raising her eyes toward the kitchen ceiling.

Laura hugged her knees and looked through the window at the roses erased by the nighttime shadows, and the neighbors' windows where the lights were starting to go out.

Nachita poured salt onto the back of her hand and ate it greedily.

"So many coyotes! The pack is getting excited," she said, her voice full of salt.

Laura sat listening for a few seconds.

"Damned animals, you should have seen them this afternoon," she said.

"As long as they don't hinder the master, or make him lose his way," Nacha said fearfully.

"If he's never been afraid of them before, why would he fear them tonight?" Laura asked, annoyed.

Nacha went closer to her mistress, to deepen the sudden intimacy that had grown between them.

"They are greater scoundrels than the Tlaxcaltecas," she said in a very low voice.

The two women were quiet, Nacha slowly devouring another handful of salt, Laura listening worriedly to the howls of the coyotes that filled the night. It was Nacha who saw him arrive, and she opened the window to him.

"Ma'am…! He's come for you…" she whispered in a voice so low only Laura could hear it.

Later, after Laura had gone with him forever, Nachita cleaned the blood from the window and shooed away the coyotes entering her century, which had just in that instant ended. Nacha looked around with her ancient eyes to be sure everything was in order: she washed the coffee cup, threw out the cigarette butts stained with red lipstick, returned the coffeepot to the cupboard, and turned out the light.

"If you ask me, Señora Laurita was not of this time, and she wasn't right for the master," she said in the morning, when she brought breakfast in to Señora Margarita.

Later she confided in Josefina, "I don't feel comfortable in the Aldama house anymore. I'm going to look for something else." And when the maid wasn't looking, Nacha left without even waiting to be paid.

THE COBBLER FROM GUANAJUATO

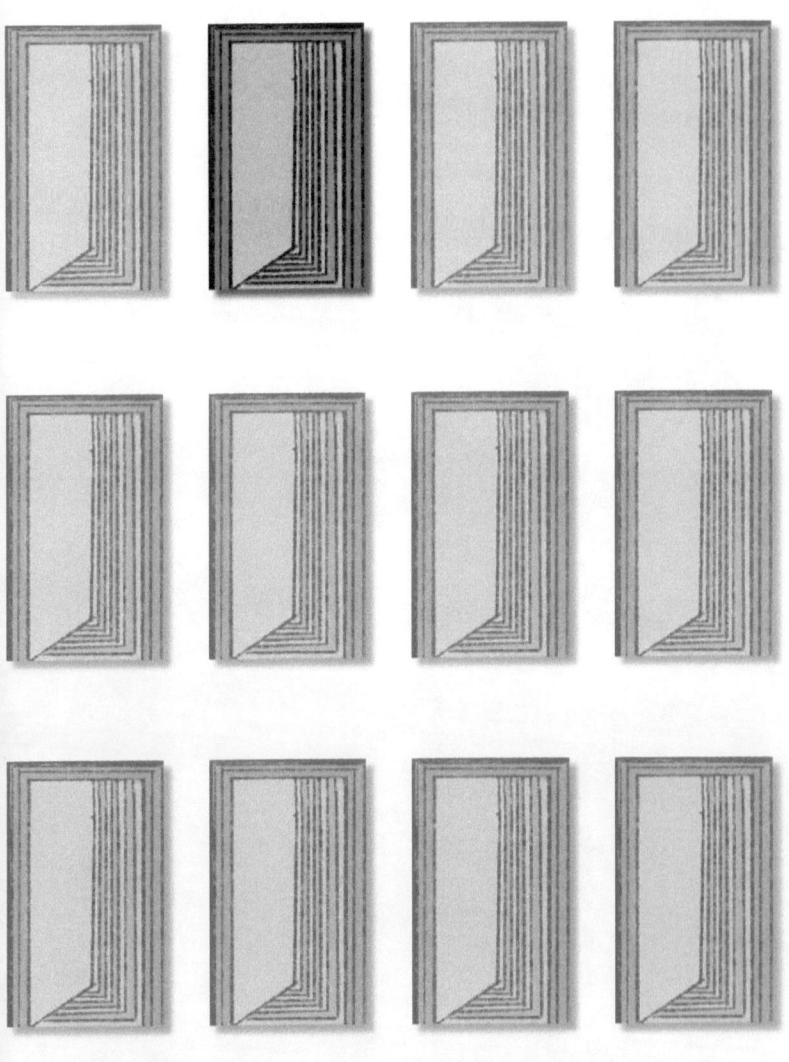

I was walking along down the street, holding Faustino by the hand; my little grandson didn't say a word, but I could well see that three days of wandering the city without food or shelter had discouraged him. "With no money, no family, and no friends, what will become of us?" I went along saying to myself, and I saw the houses and windows observing me as I passed. I was never a beggar, and the shame of hunger made me walk without looking where I stepped. The unfamiliar city is hostile, and its countless streets are indifferent to the sadness of an outsider. "What will become of us without a soul to see us?" I went along hearing Faustino's racing little footsteps, not looking at him so as not to see his hunger… "Surely his mouth is very dry. Man learns by suffering…" Or so I was walking along and saying to myself when I saw her for the first time. She was in a brand-new car, perched on the seat, in a tight embrace with a man who held her by the waist. All I could see of him was his black hair over one of her shoulders, and the arms that held her.

I said to myself, "My goodness! Around here, people kiss in the middle of the street and in the full light of day!" I noticed her slender waist beneath her white dress. The car door was open, and I saw that her legs were as bare as her arms. Faustino saw them, too. And both of us saw when she raised a hand and slapped him even as they were kissing. Offended, he jerked his head back, and then I saw no more. I couldn't stick around to watch. "Nosey old man!" they would have said, and with plenty of reason. Faustino and I went on down the street. "What a quick temper!" I said to myself, and now I say, "Pray that God will stay her hand, so she doesn't meet a bad end!" Suddenly, the new car went whizzing past us. We saw that they were struggling inside: him to hold her back, her with the door open. The car was zigzagging like a drunk. "God willing a post doesn't get in their way...!" Faustino and I went on down the avenue, which seemed to have no end. That avenue was like all the streets of Mexico City: enclosed by walls and houses, with no outlet to the countryside. The light there is very white and free of greenery, and at that midday hour, with sleepless eyes, well-walked feet, and a clear stomach, it's tiring. I've seen a lot in my eighty-two years, but nothing as desolate as Mexico City at noon. Faustino was frightened. That's what she said when she spoke to us. Because suddenly, we saw her come walking toward us. Her white dress dazzled in the sun. She seemed very excited. Her large eyes widened as she stared at us.

"You're not from here, right?"

We looked like outsiders to her, because of the coarse

cloth of our pants, our huarache sandals, and our hats burned by the sun.

"No, child."

She thought long and hard; she thinks about everything a lot, though it seems like she doesn't.

"Where are you staying?"

"Nowhere, child."

It was ugly to beg from her, and we both preferred to lower our eyes. We were ashamed of our misfortune.

"Have you eaten?"

She asked directly and without beating around the bush. Why lie, when she could see our hunger? My eyes clouded over; old age is no good for holding back tears when they want to fall.

"No, child. Neither my grandson nor I have tasted food in the three days we've been roaming these blessed streets."

I said it all for the boy. Pride must be set aside when little ones are involved.

"Three days?"

She stared at us as though we were telling lies, and then she turned to look at the cars that never cease to pass on that avenue.

"There is a lot of hunger, child! A lot of hunger. We're not the only ones who suffer from it; in my village we all have the same misfortune. That's why we've come from the countryside to seek solace in the city."

"Those government bandits…!"

She got angry like a mare, stamping her feet on the ground.

"Come."

I wasn't shamed by her charity. She gave it angrily, as if she were at fault for my sad situation. The coolness of her house was a comfort after the arid street. Her servants started to laugh when they saw us. Then their laughter stopped, and they turned serious. One of them went over to Miss Blanquita.

"Ma'am, he's called three times now, one right after the other. Nonstop, nonstop."

Miss Blanquita turned red from indignation and rested her face on her hand so as not to think. We were all silent.

"If he calls again, tell him I haven't come home…or that I died…"

She and her servants became very sad. Faustino and I pretended not to have heard anything and to not be there at all. The maids led us to a room to rest while they prepared food for us.

"What a bother we are!" I said.

"Don't worry yourself, sir, we're used to it. This is how Miss Blanquita is."

And so she is. I spent the afternoon in the kitchen chatting with them. I told them about Guanajuato and the tribulations we were going through. I wanted to repay them for the kindness of their hospitality and laughter. When it grew dark, Miss Blanquita came into the kitchen. She was quite sad. She took a seat and smoked two cigarettes without saying a word.

"Go and see Chino. Ask if he'll give us something for dinner on credit," she said suddenly.

I never would have thought that such a well-appointed house and such a finely dressed lady wouldn't have a cent for dinner. She seemed so rich!

"Money evaporates like water. It's cursed, isn't it?"

Very true that it was cursed. And I said as much to Miss Blanquita.

"Is there a lot of hunger where you're from?"

"Yes, child, very much."

Asking questions, and more questions, she had me tell her of my life, my sorrows, and the reason I had traveled to Mexico City. "I'm a cobbler by trade," I told her. "But because of all the poverty, no one in Guanajuato buys shoes anymore. That's why I collected a few pennies, which I borrowed from the loan shark, and I made a few pairs to come and sell in Mexico City, where rich people wear shoes. They turned out very pretty, with silver laces and high heels. We are miners there, and we like both gold and silver. In other times everything was gold: palaces, combs, altars, and at some houses even the bars on the windows were made of gold. But, as I said, those were other times. Now we are poor, that's why I brought my shoes here. Rosa, my oldest daughter, wrapped them up in silken paper and lent me her son Faustino to keep me company on my trip. My daughter Gertrudis prepared food for us and packed up some provisions. And one Thursday, well before dawn, we set out. At three in the morning, we took the highway and walked until midday. At that hour we sought shelter in the house of a coal merchant, who offered us his compassion, his fresh water, and his fire to heat our tortillas. We also stayed the night with him. We left in the early morning. When we said goodbye, he commended us to God and told us he would welcome us again on our return. In the nine days the trip took we made good time, and we found comfort with good people who took pity on us. On me, due to my eighty-two years. And on Faustino, my little grandson, because of his tender eight years. When we entered Mexico City, we went straight to the Villa de Guadalupe to give thanks. We spent the night in the entrance to the Villa, alongside other pilgrims who were also coming in search of solace for their hunger and sorrow. Talking with them, making conversation, one man assured me that people would certainly buy my shoes at any market.

"How lovely, he said when I showed him the shoes. I didn't quite realize that he was looking at them covetously, until the next day when I woke up without them. Faustino said to me, Let's go find them, Grandpa, he can't have gotten far.

"And that's what we did: we looked and looked without finding them. The man wasn't very tall, he wore a leather jacket, and he had very black hair and a nice laugh. But we couldn't find him. We were looking for him, without a cent to our name and no way to get back to Guanajuato, when we found you, Miss Blanquita."

Miss Blanquita looked at us sympathetically.

"And how much did your shoes cost?"

"Around about a hundred or five hundred pesos. I never knew for sure, because, as I said, I never got to sell them."

"Oh, what a bargain!"

And Miss Blanquita burst out laughing. It must be said that she doesn't do anything halfway; either she laughs a lot, or else she's very angry.

"Five hundred pesos…I'll give you that, and I'll pay for your bus tickets back to Guanajuato."

I thanked her profusely. I gave her my name along with my thanks: Loreto Rosales, at her service. And my grandson, Faustino Duque, her servant as well. Just then the maid, a curvy, good-looking woman named Josefina, returned.

"Chino said that he's already sold us a lot on credit, and he wouldn't even give me a bit of cheese."

"May he burn in hell!"

And Miss Blanquita left the kitchen uttering coarse words, she who is so refined. That night we dined on black coffee and hard tortillas with salt. But we did not grieve over it, because, as Miss Blanquita herself told us, we were all under the protection of Divine Providence. As soon as we finished our supper, they turned off the lights in the room and drew the curtains of the windows that looked onto the street. They also turned off the kitchen lights. Miss Blanquita and her maids got down on the floor by the windows, where they could look out at the street through a gap in the curtain.

"There he is, Miss Blanquita," Josefina murmured.

"See, ma'am, he's looking this way, patrolling the house…"

"The bastard, I'm going to call the police," said the lady.

"Yes, ma'am, give him a scare before he kills us."

We spied on the danger until who knows what time, because Faustino and I eventually withdrew to go to bed.

I almost didn't sleep thinking about the enemy who was stalking Miss Blanquita. I heard the hours chime: twelve, one in the morning, and still they were down there, spying on the evildoer's steps so they'd be ready. Good thing Miss Blanquita seemed quite frightened. So did Josefina and Panchita. With that thought, I slept.

"Have you had breakfast yet, Don Loretito?" the lady of the house asked me in the morning.

"Yes, child."

"Today I'll give you your money, so you can return to Guanajuato…"

And so the days began to pass, and I was ever more ashamed. Miss Blanquita didn't have a cent to her name, and I couldn't do anything for her, not even leave, because that would have offended her.

"Let me go, Miss Blanquita!"

"You're crazy, Don Loretito!"

She laughed, put on music, and danced. Nothing distressed her. She never went out, for she was very menaced. At night, she and her maids would peer out at the street.

"We're under siege!"

"Only God can help us."

During the day Josefina went to ask for things on credit. Before leaving, she spied from the balcony.

"I'll race on out before he comes and catches me."

And she soon came back with the goods on credit. While she cooked noodle soup and squash blossom quesadillas, she sang. That Josefina had a pretty voice. Panchita also sang while she made the beds and cleaned the mirrors.

Miss Blanquita would dance a little and do some embroidery. I felt just fine and no longer asked to leave. What more did I want? I was treated well and had good company. My grandson was allowed to play with the radio. I didn't even remember the city outside anymore. Someday Divine Providence would remember us and send us the money we needed. Then, with a heavy heart, I would return to Guanajuato. And I say with a heavy heart because I had grown fond of those three women: it's hard to find folks who laugh so easily. That's how my thoughts went, and that's how my days passed. One evening, as dusk was falling, someone came to the door. From my room I could hear Josefina's voice.

"I'm sorry, sir, but I can't take the package…"

"Why not?" It was a booming, masculine voice.

I heard Josefina slam the door.

"Miss Blanquita, this came for you!" Josefina called anxiously.

"Idiot! Why did you accept it?"

I heard them unwrapping the package.

"See? See? Look! Look!"

I didn't dare poke my head in to see what had come. Josefina entered, very upset.

"She's going to get killed…he's going to kill her…"

A while later I saw Faustino playing with two broken dolls. They were both dressed as brides and their white gowns were ripped to shreds, their blonde tresses nearly torn out.

"Where did you find these, boy?"

"They were there, on the floor."

We asked for needles and a little thread, and we began to repair them. That's what we were doing when a knock came again at the door. I prepared for a fight; I had to be good for something in spite of my eighty-two years.

"Do you want to kill her?" Josefina shouted.

"So her grave will flower!" I heard the same booming voice.

"Ma'am...! Miss Blanquita."

I went out to see, too, and there they were, strewn over the ground: who knows how many red roses.

"He threw them, ma'am, when I wouldn't take them!"

"Flowers on the floor of my house, what a bad omen! What a bad omen!" Miss Blanquita cried.

All red from indignation, she picked them up, then opened the window and threw them onto the street. Josefina helped her. Panchita, on the other hand, grabbed a dozen and hid them in one of the bathrooms.

"Come and see, Don Loretito."

Miss Blanquita led me to the balcony. Night had fallen, and the flowers glittered like confetti under the streetlights. A pity how the cars were driving over them. We went back inside when we saw they were all crushed. After a while someone came to the door again, but this time the knocking was very hard, as if the person wanted to knock it down. It seemed to me that they were kicking it or pounding the butt of a gun against it.

"I'll get it, Josefina!"

We saw Miss Blanquita go by like a flash; she was enraged.

Then we didn't hear anything. Cautiously, we came out of the room. The floor of the hall had another bunch of red roses, and the door to the street was wide open.

"He took her!" Josefina screamed.

"Yes, he took her," Faustino repeated.

The four of us found ourselves quite frightened. God only knew where she'd gone and if she would someday return. We were just about to say something, when Miss Blanquita reappeared to us. She was very disheveled, with her hair hanging limply over her face and her white dress torn.

"He ran me over with the car…! Pour me a tequila…"

The lady dropped into a silken chair. Her knees were scraped. Josefina cleaned the blood from her legs, fixed her hair, and wiped her face with a handkerchief. Panchita gave us all a generous pour of tequila.

"Go ahead, Don Loretito, for the fright."

With Miss Blanquita, a person goes from one shock to the next. She downed her tequila and seemed to recover. Then she stood up and went to the phone.

"Do me the favor of coming to the corner where my house is. Let's see if you're brave enough to say it to my face… I'll expect you in ten minutes."

After a while she came into the kitchen all resolute, now in a different dress. She smiled at us, but I could tell she was extremely mad. She searched and searched among the knives, but then decided on a hammer. She put it under her arm with the head up and the handle close to her body, and she held it with her elbow. It looked like she was unarmed.

She is crafty and knows what she's doing!

"I'll be right back."

She blew us a kiss with her free hand and left. The girls stared at me. "Old fool, what are you good for?" I could read their thoughts.

"I'm going to follow her...you never know..."

I went outside, where I hadn't set foot in many days. There were just as many cars at night as at midday, and the street was filled with the reflections of their headlights. They kept me from seeing where Miss Blanquita was. Finally, I caught sight of her on the opposite sidewalk. There was a very tall, brawny man beside her. They didn't seem to be talking, just looking at each other: sizing each other up. I slipped between the cars, and, very cautiously, I approached.

"Follow me!"

"Not here," cried the lady.

The big man turned to look all around, searching.

"You must have your Indians protecting you," he said fearfully.

"Follow me."

The lady started to walk and the man followed her, looking, looking all around, distrustfully. His eyes never landed on me. Who notices me? No one! No one knows how to look at a poor man. Plus, I know how to walk so no one sees me. I was taught as a child. We went down some streets with yards and no people. Very dark streets! I slipped between the trees and the few lampposts. I also pressed my back against doorways and metal bars. Miss Blanquita was very far ahead, walking without turning around, keeping her arms close to her body, hiding the weapon, very upright. She turned left and he followed. I pressed close to the corner and peeked out. His back was to me. She was approaching him.

"Now we're alone, tell me again what you said."

"What I said…? What did I say?" asked the man, frightened.

"Repeat what you said!"

"You are bad. Very bad…"

And after making his complaint, the man turned around. No sooner was his back to her than Miss Blanquita took out her hammer, raised it with both hands, and brought it down sharply onto the nape of his neck. The head of the hammer fell onto the sidewalk and bounced into the middle of the street. That's how hard the blow was! The man took a few stumbling steps. In the light of the streetlamps, I saw his eyes roll back. As though drunk, he went into the street and fumbled around for the hammer's head, picked it up, and managed to throw it into a yard. Then he collapsed into a seated position on the ground, clutching his skull. Miss Blanquita went over to him to finish the job with the hammer's handle. But the man snatched it away and threw it into the yard as well.

"Traitor…! You hit me from behind…"

She was angry at having left her enemy alive. She was brave, because the enemy was quite strapping; he was a head taller than her and weighed twice as much. As he sat there, I could see large hands and a broad back. The lady looked at him for a while and then turned back toward her house. The man got up to follow her. They passed very close to me without seeing me. I followed them. "As long as she has the advantage over him, I won't interfere. She's very strong and doesn't need me to defend her," I went along saying to myself, and then we reached the last little street, the one that leads to her avenue. There, she stopped to think—guess what about! There was a tobacco shop open near the corner.

"Buy me some cigarettes!" she ordered.

I remembered that she hadn't smoked since the morning, because Chino wouldn't stand her the Monte Carlos.

"Yes, my love…"

I heard her enemy give that answer. And, cautiously, he stopped at the door of the shop, where he could keep watch over the side street and prevent her from reaching the avenue. He was blocking her path. She looked at him and backed up slowly, very slowly. When the enemy went inside to pay for the cigarettes, Miss Blanquita looked all around, searching for an escape in the dark little street, but all escape routes would take her past the shop door. She looked up to the sky and found the branches of the ash tree. Without hesitating, she climbed the tree like a cat and disappeared into the dark foliage. The man emerged with the cigarettes in his hand and didn't see her anywhere. But he wasn't discouraged: alert, he went up the street, looking all around, scrutinizing the yards, the gates, the entrances of houses. Then down the street. Then up the street again, searching; then down the street again. I sat on the curb, lowered my hat, and pretended to be asleep as I watched him: up the street, down the street. Miss Blanquita's tree was very still. And the man kept going, upstreet, downstreet, looking all around. "The bastard knows she has not left this godforsaken place, and he's blocking her path." More than an hour went by. The shop closed, and the man kept going up the street, down the street. No doubt Miss Blanquita was watching him, and that's why she didn't move.

"Toss me a cigarette!" she shouted suddenly from the branches of the ash tree. I have always said that both man and woman are always betrayed by their vices.

"Where, Blanca, where?" asked the man, spinning around like a top.

"Up here."

"Where?"

"In the ash tree!"

The enemy grabbed the trunk of the tree and laughed so hard that his laughter spread to me. He laughed so much that it took some work to throw her the cigarettes, since she didn't want to come down.

"Go away, so I can go back to my house!"

"I want to see your face!"

"Impossible. Only my friends can see it."

"How much does your face cost? I'll buy it!"

"Five hundred pesos!"

"The same amount you asked me for?"

"The same! I owe it to the little cobbler from Guanajuato."

I stopped laughing. The little cobbler from Guanajuato was me, Loreto Rosales. I lowered my head. I didn't want anyone to see my face. I was ashamed that I, Loreto Rosales, could have put a lady in the position of taking a hammer to kill the evil man who refused her—five hundred pesos!

"And just where is your little cobbler, so I can give it to him?"

"In a secret place, where you won't see him."

She really must not have seen me. I approached the corner all hunched over. I passed by the shop with its closed doors. I turned onto the avenue and reached the house. I went inside and grabbed Faustino, and then we took the road back to Guanajuato. It took us eleven days, because at first I couldn't find the way out of Mexico City. I went without even saying goodbye, because there are times when it's more polite not to say goodbye. In the eleven days of walking, I was comforted by the thought that by leaving, I was freeing Miss Blanquita from prison. It's been seven days now since I arrived back home. But I haven't been able to rest easy. Last night I dreamed of Miss Blanquita, standing at the Benito Juárez Hemicycle and searching for me. Maybe she needs me. That's why, bright and early, I headed out on the road back to Mexico City. At a good pace, Faustino and I will reach it in nine days, and then we'll see what we need to do for her. Ultimately, as long as she has the advantage, I won't interfere… Although with Miss Blanquita, you never know, you just never know…

WHAT TIME IS IT...?

"What time is it, Señor Brunier?"

Lucía's brown eyes briefly recovered the lost wonder of childhood.

Brunier was expecting the question. He looked at his wristwatch and, pronouncing each syllable so Lucía would understand the answer, said, "It's nine forty-four."

"Still three minutes to go...what a long day! It's lasted a lifetime. Will God grant me those three minutes?"

Brunier looked at her for a few seconds: reclining on the bed, her wide-open eyes looking toward that long day that had been her entire life.

"God will grant you many years," he said, leaning over her and looking into her brown eyes: withered leaves that a cold wind was sweeping far, far away from that cramped chamber.

"Someone is coming into this room...love is for this world and for the next. What time is it, Señor Brunier?"

Brunier again leaned over to look into those tea-colored

eyes that were starting to grow dim, spinning through the air like leaves.

"Nine forty-seven, Madame Lucía," he said in a respectful voice, looking her in the eyes, which now seemed like they could be strewn on any old sidewalk.

"Nine forty-seven," he repeated superstitiously, wishing she could hear him. But she was motionless, freed now of the time, stretched out in the bed of a cheap room in a luxury hotel.

Brunier took her wrist, checking for a pulse that he knew wasn't there. With a steady hand, he lowered her eyelids. The room filled with a deep silence that reached from ceiling to floor and from wall to wall. Her peach-colored chiffon scarf lay atop a tattered suitcase. He picked it up and spread it over the body, which made only a small bulge beneath it on the bed. Sepia hair formed a tousled blotch under the gauzy fabric.

Brunier dropped into an armchair and stared at the shining windowpanes. Outside, pale automobiles filled and emptied with noisy young people. How many years now had he been there, stuffed into that green-and-gold uniform, keeping watch at the hotel entrance? Twenty-three. And thus his life had passed. It seemed to him he had opened the door only to evildoers. The troop was endless, and the "Good mornings," "Good afternoons," and "Good nights" were endless as well. Only Madame Mitre had said to him upon entering, "What's the time?" He remembered it so clearly: she had come in followed by two bellhops carrying her suitcases. She wasn't so young, perhaps she had turned thirty already. Still, as she passed, she smiled a shameless smile at him. "Ladies don't smile like that, only boys do," Brunier thought to himself. And to top it all off, this lady had winked at him. He was disconcerted. This guest wore a broad, peach-colored chiffon scarf around her neck, its ends floating behind her like wings. One end of the scarf got caught in a door, and the smiling foreigner took a step back when she felt herself being strangled by the gauze. Brunier hurried to free the garment, and then bowed respectfully before the traveler.

"Thank you, thank you!" the lady said over and over in a strong foreign accent.

Brunier bowed again, ready to withdraw. The foreigner stopped him, smiling.

"What is your name?"

"Brunier," he replied, embarrassed by the lady's lack of discretion.

"What time is it, Señor Brunier?"

Brunier looked at his wristwatch.

"It's six-ten, ma'am."

"The flight from London lands at nine forty-seven, right?"

"I believe so…" the doorman replied.

"Still three hours and thirty-seven minutes to go," said the stranger in a tragic voice.

The foreign lady strode across the hotel lobby. Her short coat revealed two long, thin legs that walked as though they were not used to crossing salons, but rather to running fast over plains. She registered at the hotel as Lucía Mitre, accepted her key, and coolly commanded, "Reserve room

410 for Señor Gabriel Cortina, who will arrive today from London at nine forty-seven."

Room 410 was beside room 412, the number she had been assigned.

For several days, Madame Mitre ate lunch and dinner in her room. No one saw her go out. Room 410 remained empty. Amid the busy life of a hotel, with so many people going in and out, so many parties, so many automobiles pulling up to its doors, these trivial facts passed unnoticed. Only Brunier watched the guests attentively as they entered and exited, hoping to catch another glimpse of the woman with the peach-colored scarf who had winked at him and asked the time. Discreetly, he asked around among the maids and waiters.

"What's that? The South American? She's crazy. She gets all dressed up, then sits in a chair and asks, What time is it?"

Marie Claire, after imitating the foreigner's gestures and voice, laughed heartily.

"She's obsessed! With me as well, she only asks what time it is," said Albert, the waiter who delivered her breakfast.

"Something is wrong…" said Brunier, thoughtful.

"She's waiting for her lover…" Marie Claire cried with another catty laugh.

Brunier listened to these confidences and went on watching over the grand main entrance. Two months passed. The hotel management asked Madame Mitre if she planned to keep room 410 reserved.

"Of course! Señor Gabriel Cortina will arrive today on the nine forty-seven plane," she replied with aplomb.

"She's an eccentric!" said the management.

"Rich people are allowed to be eccentric. What does she care about those francs, when back in her own country she has a hundred thousand horses and three hundred thousand cows?" replied Mademoiselle Ivonne in a bitter voice as she turned from the account book to join in the conversation.

"All South Americans have very good cows and very bad manners. Since they lack ideas, they're full of manias," said Monsieur Gilbert, peering down from atop his stiff neck.

Madame Mitre did not have so many cows, and at the end of the third month she didn't have money to pay the latest hotel bill. Gilbert went up to her room. She opened the door with a smile, ushered him in, and offered him a seat.

"Ma'am, I'm sorry, I'm truly distraught, but…you'll have to move to a different hotel."

"Move?" asked the lady, astonished.

Gilbert was silent. Then he nodded gravely.

"I can't move. I'm here to wait for Señor Gabriel Cortina. He's arriving tonight, on the nine forty-seven plane. What will he say if I'm not here? It would be a catastrophe. A real catastrophe!"

Gilbert was very sorry. The hotel bill had not been paid.

"If I understand correctly, Madame has nothing with which to pay the bill."

"Money? No, I don't have anything," the lady said, throwing her head back and laughing heartily.

"Nothing?" Gilbert asked, terrified.

"Nothing! Properly nothing," she assured him, still laughing.

Gilbert looked at her without understanding. Truly, this woman's confession was terrifying.

"Why do you doubt his word, when he told me he would be arriving today on the nine forty-seven plane…?" she asked.

"No, it's not that I doubt it…" Gilbert said, disconcerted.

Madame Mitre looked at him for a while with her tea-colored eyes. Then she seemed to grow nervous, wringing her hands and bringing her face very close to Monsieur Gilbert's.

"What time is it…?" she asked anxiously.

"Four oh-five," the man replied, almost in spite of himself.

The afternoons were very short now, and the gray, cold dusk spilled in through the windows. Gilbert turned on a lamp that was on a side table, and its pink light shone onto Madame Mitre's pale face. It was difficult to tell that cheerful, delicate woman that she would have to vacate the room, and immediately at that. He looked at her bravely.

"Ma'am…!"

She turned to him, smiling that peasant-boy smile of hers, and winked.

"Yes, sir…"

"If you could, at the very least, leave something…"

"Something?" she asked, startled. She uncrossed her legs.

"Yes, something valuable," said Gilbert impatiently. Why must it fall to him to come and say these stupid things to Madame Mitre?

Lucía Mitre rested her elbows on her knees and her face on her hands, then stared at him as if she didn't understand his request. Gilbert stayed silent. He couldn't think of a single word to add.

"Oh! Something valuable?" Lucía repeated, as though to herself. She half-closed her eyes and recrossed her legs. Suddenly resolute, she raised her hands to the nape of her neck and removed her necklace of several strands of pearls.

"How about this?" she asked, holding the pearls toward him. Gilbert saw their iridescent sheen and seemed to relax.

"They are very expensive… How I begged for them. You see? No one knows who they're begging for. If Ignacio only knew…" she added, as though to herself.

Monsieur Gilbert didn't know what to say. Lucía held out the necklace with a sweeping gesture.

"Ignacio is my husband," she said in explanation.

"Your husband…?" Gilbert asked as he accepted the precious object.

"Yes, my husband…"

Madame Mitre sat staring into space, as if the word *husband* had transported her to a hollow world.

"It's a very complicated story. Aren't complications just odious, Señor….?"

"Gilbert," her interlocutor replied almost mechanically.

"Gilbert," she completed her sentence.

Lucía's words sounded unreal in the pink-lit room. Her voice emerged slowly and seemed not to be directed at anyone. Her just-uttered sentences spun fragile through the air and tumbled soundlessly onto the carpet. Lucía looked at Gilbert so he would not forget what she was about to say.

"Now you understand why Gabriel Cortina is arriving

tonight on the nine forty-seven plane, right?"

Gilbert said nothing and put the necklace away until later, when he could examine it alone.

Word spread among the hotel employees: "Madame Mitre gave up a fabulous pearl necklace so she can keep waiting for her lover." The rumor reached Monsieur Brunier's ears. It had been five months since the afternoon when Madame Lucía had winked at him, and Brunier, though he hadn't seen her again, had not forgotten her. He was always on the lookout for her long, floating scarf and welcoming smile. Room 410 had been occupied by countless travelers, all headed for the Austrian mountains or the sunshine of Spain and Portugal, and Madame Mitre remained invisible in room 412 of the hotel. Brunier was uneasy. He knew that sooner or later the lady would run through her pearls, one by one, and then she would be out on the street. This idea tormented him.

"Mademoiselle Ivonne, how many pearls does Madame Mitre have left?" asked Brunier, fearful of the reply.

"Twenty-two," said Ivonne.

"And then?"

"Then, hup!" Ivonne replied, snapping her fingers.

"I must have a talk with her," Brunier said thoughtfully.

"She won't listen to you. She's waiting for her lover, and her lover isn't coming," Ivonne said with conviction.

"She is acting like a child," Brunier insisted.

Sunday afternoon, Brunier went up to room 412. He smoothed his hair before knocking, feeling that he was embarking upon an important mission and he must not fail.

Lucía Mitre opened the door. She greeted him with a smile, invited him in, and offered him a seat with her usual sweeping and happy gestures.

"Really, she has excellent manners. It's just that she wouldn't listen to me. The only thing I managed to do was convince her to move to room 101, since there she'll get two days per pearl. Early tomorrow morning I'll bring down her luggage," Brunier said later.

"This story is starting to make me nervous," said Albert.

"And this supposed Gabriel, just where *is* he?" Marie Claire said with a sigh.

"Maybe he doesn't exist. Maybe she made him up," said Mauricio, one of the elevator operators.

"It's certainly possible. Otherwise, he'd have given some sign of life by now," Marie Claire agreed.

Later on, Ivonne ran into Monsieur Brunier in the locker room. She had caught wind of Mauricio's theory and wanted to talk to the old doorman about it, since he seemed so interested in the foreigner.

"You know, Brunier, that she has never received a letter from anywhere in the world?"

"And doesn't she ask if she has any correspondence?" Brunier asked, deep in thought.

"No, she doesn't mention it. She only asks about the time. She says her watch is very slow," Ivonne explained eagerly.

"But she must have lived somewhere before. Don't tell me she just appeared out of nowhere, right in the middle of Paris!"

Lucía Mitre lived in room 101 for many days. Only the

maids saw her. She ate lunch and dinner in her room and never spoke with anyone. Then Monsieur Gilbert went to visit her a second time. Once again, he had to ask her to leave the hotel. But Lucía smilingly retrieved some diamond earrings from her jewelry box and handed them over to her visitor.

Brunier went up to room 101. He wanted to convince Madame Mitre to do something humiliating: move to a cheaper hotel. That way, her diamond earrings would turn into many days.

"Many days...? But Gabriel will be here today on the plane that arrives at nine forty-seven. Why are you all in such a hurry...? Have you never seen someone spend the whole day waiting for her lover?"

"Yes...one day," Brunier said.

"So...? What time is it?" she asked.

"Twelve-thirty in the afternoon," Brunier replied, look-ing at her in desperation.

"Well, in nine hours and seventeen minutes, Gabriel will arrive..."

Lucía lowered her head, seeming tired. She looked at the tips of her shoes and smoothed the pleats of her silk, peach-colored skirt. Then she smiled faintly at the doorman, who felt ashamed. Nothing he could say to her was valid, because Lucía Mitre was circling like a moth around a flame that he could not see, but that was there, in that very room, blinding her.

"Of course, Señor Brunier, time has turned to stone... Each minute that passes is as huge as a giant boulder. New cities are built and they flourish, fall, and disappear, and cities and minutes go passing by; and the minute of nine forty-seven will arrive once all the stone minutes and huge cities that come before the minute I'm waiting for have passed. When that instant arrives, the city of birds will arise from this pile of minutes and stones…"

"Yes, ma'am," Brunier said respectfully.

"I'm very tired…very tired…it's the stones," added Lucía, looking at the doorman with exhausted eyes. Then, with apparent effort, she winked at him and smiled her open, boyish smile. Brunier wanted to smile back, but he was overcome by an inexplicable sadness that paralyzed him.

"When I was a little girl, Señor Brunier, time flowed like music through a flute. Back then I only frolicked and played, I didn't wait. If we adults would only play, we would put an end to the stones inside the clock. Back then, love was outside the walls of my house, waiting for me like a big bonfire, all gold, and when my father opened the door and told me, Go outside, Lucía! I ran toward the flames; my vocation was to be a salamander…"

Brunier realized then that Madame Lucía was bewitched. But by whom, and what for?

"And you, Señor Brunier, how many salamanders have you had?" Lucía asked with interest, as if she suddenly remembered that she ought to speak more about her interlocutor and less about herself.

"Two, but they were true salamanders, they didn't get burned in the fire," replied Brunier.

After the doorman's visit, the lady was even quieter.

She never rang the bell or asked for anything. They ended up sending her nearly empty trays. Monsieur Gilbert visited her from time to time and took away her treasures one by one. He was troubled by that constant presence in the hotel's cheapest room. The spring passed with its bouquets of snow covering the chestnuts; summer shed its leaves into a yellow autumn, winter returned with its steaming kettles, and Lucía Mitre continued to ask the time, locked away in her room. Monsieur Gilbert bore her very much in mind.

"Ma'am, wouldn't it be appropriate to write to your husband?"

"My husband…? What for?"

"So he can do something for you…so that he can come and get you. A Mexican man, wherever he may be, is always a gentleman."

"Oh! Yes, he is the best of men. I will always be grateful to him, Señor Gilbert. If you only knew…we lived in marriage for eight years…I will never forget the nights I spent in the immense bedroom of his house. My mother-in-law heard me cry and came in wearing a Japanese kimono…"

Madame Mitre was silent, as if she could hear the approaching footsteps of that woman she was naming for the very first time. Gilbert glanced toward the door; he had the impression that someone wrapped in Eastern garb was soundlessly entering the room. Madame Mitre covered her face with her hands and started to sob. Gilbert stood.

"Madame! Please…"

"The room was huge, full of mirrors, and I felt very lonely. That angered my mother-in-law… Does it seem very bad to you, Señor Gilbert?"

"No, no, it seems natural," Gilbert replied, blushing.

"I saw Ignacio in the dining room. The day he wrote the letter I was very surprised, because he could have told me over lunch. Then I realized it was the best way for him to tell me something so delicate. Do you want to read it?"

Gilbert didn't know what to say. Madame Mitre stood up quickly and rummaged in her suitcase for a small coffer of strongly scented wood. When she opened it, she inhaled the perfume with delight and cried:

"It's from Olinalá!"

Then she took out a letter clearly written long ago and read many times over. She handed it to Gilbert with that gesture of hers, sweeping and smiling, which she always used when she had to hand something over, be it her pearls, her earrings, or her letter.

"Read it, please!"

Gilbert ran his eyes over the letter without understanding a thing. It was written in Spanish, and he could only decipher the signature: "Ignacio." He nodded as if he understood what that letter said, then he folded it carefully and started to put it away like he had the pearls, so he could ask someone to translate it later. But Lucía Mitre held out her hand, and he had no choice but to give it back to her.

"You see?" she said simply. Then she got to her feet, reached for a match, and lit the paper on fire. Gilbert could not stop her, and the letter writhed in the flames until it became a little black cloth that crumpled into pieces.

"It's no good now, right?" she asked in amazement.

"No, it's no good now," Gilbert agreed, disheartened. He was sure that the burned letter held the secret of Lucía Mitre.

"What time is it? How long until nine forty-seven?"

"Four hours and twenty-three minutes," Gilbert said mournfully.

"Four hours...!"

"While you wait for nine o'clock, why not go out and take a stroll around Paris? If you could only see how beautiful the quays are, full of books, people walking..."

"A stroll...? No, I can't. I'm going to fix myself up a little... I'm so nervous," she said, anxiously touching her face.

Gilbert took in her sunken cheeks and thin, trembling hands.

"You are very beautiful, Madame Mitre," he said, convinced that tragedy beautifies its characters. The light enveloping the woman before him was a light that fed off of her. Her whole being burned inside some invisible, luminous flames. He had the impression that soon he would see her no more. He admired the charred bones of her cheeks and translucent fingers. When, and how, and why had she entered that beautiful, suicidal dimension? He felt vulgar beside this peach-dressed lady who was transmuting a little more each day into an incandescent substance that was forbidden to him.

"I couldn't stay in Ignacio's house after that letter... I remember how on the evening of the dinner, the silk on the dining-room walls burned in tiny flames, and how the flowers on the table smelled fresh in a way you only find in gardens. When I saw Ignacio and Emilia's hands caressing each other on the tablecloth, they seemed like the unfamiliar hands of strangers. In that moment I went to live in another palace, though it seemed like I went on sleeping in the bedroom of Ignacio's house. In the nights after my mother-in-law's visit Gabriel would come in... Have you been to Mexico? Well, Gabriel is like Mexico, full of mountains and immense valleys... There is always sun and the trees don't change their leaves, but only their shades of green..."

Madame Mitre sat there searching for those suns shining down on the treetops in her country. Gilbert left her in the company of her ghosts. "Her husband and her lover both betrayed her," he said to himself, and he went to his office feeling responsible for the woman's fate. During the two more months that she lived in the hotel, Gilbert refused to talk about her.

"Please! Don't talk to me about Madame Mitre... She gives me the shivers."

Now Lucía Mitre was covered in her gauzy, peach-colored scarf. An ancient and chivalrous rage overcame Brunier. "Poor thing!" he said to himself, thinking of Gabriel. "Poor thing!" he repeated, remembering Ignacio. He would have to let Monsieur Gilbert know what had just happened in room 101.

The period divans and armchairs upholstered in pastel silks, the mirrors, the bouquets of wildflowers and the honey-colored rugs, all gave him the feeling of entering the warm center of gold. He looked at the couples reflected in the lighted mirrors, sliding fragilely along invisible, perfumed pathways toward loves that would perhaps only last a few hours. They looked like beautiful tigers sniffing at intricate twists and turns, and he had the feeling that some of those fleeting characters would end up just like Lucía, clinging to an unrecoverable minute.

Brunier went over to Gilbert, who, standing all rosy and decked out in his impeccable jacket, was smiling at one of those chosen couples. Brunier waited a few minutes.

"Madame Lucía has just died," he announced, without betraying any emotion.

"What's that you say?" asked Gilbert, adopting the most inexpressive countenance he could manage.

"I said that Madame Lucía Mitre has just died," Brunier repeated without a change in his bearing.

"How sad!" Gilbert cried in a low voice. Then he smilingly attended to a guest who was asking where to find the bar.

"I shall call the police. We must keep the other guests from realizing what has happened."

"She died at exactly nine forty-seven," Brunier said, trying to make his voice sound natural.

Gilbert started to say something, but was distracted by a guest who came up to the desk. The man was young and carried a tennis racket in his hand, his face sun-tanned and smiling. In a playful tone, he explained that eleven months ago, a friend of his had reserved room 410 for him. He didn't know if the reservation had been made in the name of his friend, Lucía Mitre, or in his, Gabriel Cortina.

"But it's the same either way," he explained with a smile.

Gilbert was astonished and didn't know what to say. He

checked the key rack and saw that room 410 was empty. He took the key and handed it to the young man, who was absentmindedly tapping his racket against the desk.

Gilbert and Brunier, both speechless with surprise, watched as Gabriel Cortina walked off toward the elevators. He toyed with the key as he went, oblivious to their sadness. His flannel pants and sport coat gave him a boyish, American elegance. The two men looked at each other in consternation. They deliberated a few moments and decided that they would explain what had happened to the newcomer once the police arrived.

"It's a disaster!"

"A real disaster!"

At ten-thirty that night, three well-dressed men crossed the hotel lobby along with Brunier and Gilbert. The five men went up to room 410, intending to tell Gabriel Cortina what had happened. They knocked gently at his door. When no one responded to their repeated knocking, they decided to open the door with the master key. They found the room empty and untouched. Brunier and Gilbert looked at each other in shock, but they remembered the guest had carried no baggage except for his racket. They looked around for that racket, to no avail. Then they called the housekeepers, but none of them had seen the young man they were looking for. The three policemen checked the bathroom and closets. Everything was in order: no one had entered that room. Perplexed, the five men went down to the administrative office; not there, either, did any of the staff, not even Ivonne, remember that particular guest's arrival. The key to room 410 was hanging on the rack, unmoved. Gilbert and Brunier argued heatedly with the administrative staff over Gabriel Cortina's presence in the hotel. The policemen ordered searches that were fruitless, for the cheerful young man with the tennis racket did not turn up anywhere in the hotel. He had disappeared without a trace. After much discussion, they adopted the theory that they had fallen prey to a hallucination.

"It was the wish that he would come," Monsieur Gilbert had to concede, melancholic and defeated.

"Yes, that must be what happened. We both loved her," admitted Brunier.

The three policemen were moved by what had happened. One of them was from Brittany, and told of similar things happening in his land.

Somberly, the five men went to Lucía Mitre's room to finish their sad task. When they entered the room, the policemen removed their hats and leaned respectfully over the lady's body.

Brunier, solemn, pointed to the foot of the bed.

"There it is!" he said in a faint voice.

His four companions saw the white racket that had been carelessly tossed at the foot of Lucía Mitre's bed. They launched again into a search for the young man who was its owner, but their search was futile, since the cheerful guest tanned by the American sun never appeared again at the Prince Hotel.

Gilbert leaned one last time over the countenance of Lucía Mitre, who had also left the hotel forever, for nothing of her remained in her face.

THE WEEK OF COLORS

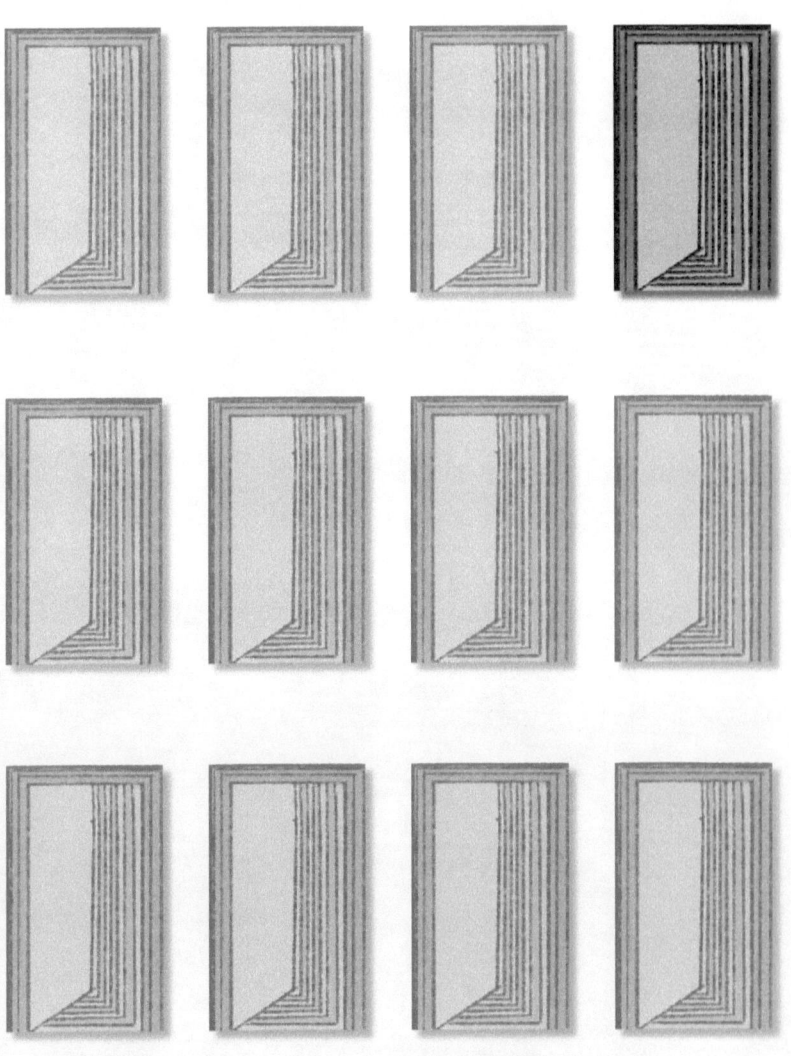

Don Flor hit Sunday until he drew blood, and Friday also emerged from that beating all bruised.

After confiding this, Candelaria bit her lips and went on pounding the sheets against the white rocks in the laundry. Her somber words broke away from the racket of water and suds and went buzzing away through the branches. The clothes were as white as the morning.

"And then?" asked Tefa.

Evita wanted to hear the rest of the conversation, but Rutilio called Tefa's name and she left the laundry room.

"What were you talking about, Candelaria?" the girl ventured to ask.

"Nothing your bratty little ears should be hearing."

All morning long, Candelaria went on flogging the white clothes against the white stones. Evita couldn't get a single word more from the washerwoman's mouth. The child waited for a long time, but in vain. The maid didn't even deign to look at her, absorbed as she was in her work and her song.

"What day is today?" Eva asked at lunchtime.

"Friday," her father replied.

"Hmm!" she said, incredulous.

The weeks didn't happen in the order her father believed. There could be three Sundays together, or four Mondays in a row. There could also be a Monday, Tuesday, Wednesday, Thursday, Friday, Saturday, and Sunday, but that was a coincidence. A real coincidence! It was much more likely that from Monday we would jump straight to Friday, and from Friday we'd go back to Tuesday.

"I wish it could always be Thursday," said Leli.

"I want it to be Tuesday," her sister replied.

Thursday and Tuesday were the best days.

"We've had five Fridays in a row now," said Leli, with an expression of distaste.

Her father looked at her.

"It's a disgrace that you still don't know the days of the week."

"But we do know them," Evita protested.

The purple, silent Fridays filled the house with cracks. The girls saw their broken walls and backed away in fear. They'd run out to the pool, and, to avoid the sight of dust, they dove into the water.

"Get out of there, your skin is getting pruned!"

They were pulled out of the water and made to sit at the table.

Fridays were days of thirst. During the nights, the sound of the broken walls kept them awake.

"You think tomorrow will be Thursday?"

The next day was Friday once again. The walls were still standing, held up by the last little piece of Thursday.

"Rutilio, what day is today?"

"Why do you want to know that, when any day is good for dying?"

That wasn't true. There were days that were better for dying. Tuesday was thin and transparent. If they died on a Tuesday, they would see through its Chinese-paper walls to the other days, the ones ahead and the ones behind. If they died on a Thursday, they would remain on a golden disk turning like a merry-go-round, and they would see all the days from a distance.

"Dad, what day is today?"

"Sunday."

"That's what the guitar calendar says, but it's not true."

"That's what the calendar says because that's what it *should* say. There's an order, and the days are part of that order."

"Hmm…! I don't think so," said the girl.

Her father started to laugh. Whenever he was wrong he laughed, pushed back their bangs, looked at their foreheads, laughed again, and then took a sip of coffee.

"The man doesn't know anything," said Evita.

"Let's go see Don Flor…"

King Philip II of Spain heard them from his portrait.

"Shh! He's listening…"

They looked at him, hanging on the wall dressed in black, listening to them whisper beside the little table where they were eating custard, near the balcony curtains.

No one ever saw Don Flor. The people who talked with him came from very far away, and only "when they had sorrows." Eva and Leli snuck out of their house to go climb the hill with giant sunflowers. From their strategic height, sitting on the ground, they could see the patio and corral of Don Flor's house. There was so much light that they could reach out their hands and touch the house, the patio, and the corral. From the hill they could see stewpots, stones, chairs, and ixtle. The house was round and painted white, and it looked like a dovecote. It had all the colors inside, but they only found that out later. Don Flor didn't wear white like other men, nor did he wear pants. His garment was long, the color of bougainvillea, and looked like a tunic. He wore his hair cut in a bob, just like the girls, and in the afternoons he sat out on the patio or in the courtyard of his house to weave baskets and chat with the Days. From the hill, the girls watched him weave the rattan and white ixtles. All the days were different colors. Sometimes the week was incomplete, and Don Flor chatted only with Wednesday and Sunday. Sometimes he was with Monday four times in a row.

"Why so much talking? Come inside, dinner's getting cold!"

Friday, peering out the window that looked onto the corral, called to Don Flor and Monday. Eva and Leli remembered that they had to go back to their own house. It was growing dark, and they hurried down from the hill and into town.

"It's been Monday for the past three days," said Evita.

"Did you two go to Don Flor's house? You'll be cursed! Don't you know he isn't Catholic? I'm going to tell your parents."

Candelaria got very angry when she heard they were going to see Don Flor. He, on the other hand, didn't know, and went on nonchalantly walking around his corral and weaving baskets with his dark hands. The Days sat in a circle on mats. That ring of Days looked very pretty. The week together was like a rainbow, and it came out even when there was no rain. One day Don Flor went over to Thursday, who was weaving white ixtle, and placed an orange nopal flower in the end of her black braid. The flower was the color of her dress. Eva and Leli stayed sitting on the hill all afternoon, in spite of the heat that came down from the sky and rose from the earth. They couldn't take their eyes from the orange flower in that black braid. The hairy sunflowers were withered, and instead of offering shade, they amplified the heat as if they were made of wool.

"Too bad we don't have black braids!"

At night, their illuminated house shone like the orange flower in Thursday's black braid.

"Today is Thursday!" they announced, radiant.

Philip II looked at them disapprovingly. It seemed to them like he wanted to smack them.

"They get the days mixed up. They're bewitched..." sighed Candelaria, handing them the little basket of cakes.

The maid crossed her arms and looked at the girls for a long time. She, too, shone black in the orange light of Thursday. The girls noisily chewed their pastries.

"Our Lord Jesus Christ is going to take your eyes, for looking at things you shouldn't."

"Our Lord Jesus Christ doesn't scare us."

"What are you saying, you wicked children? Are you also unafraid of mistaking the days?"

They didn't answer and went on eating their cakes. Our Lord could also make mistakes, and he could have named the days wrong. Impossible for him to know everything. After that day, there were many Thursdays, round and orange. Little by little the last Thursday turned red and Sunday came in once again, without Our Lord ever taking their eyes. Nor had Candelaria told on them to their parents, and Philip II looked at them with anger but no words.

"Want to go see what day he takes out today?"

They ran off toward the hill of sunflowers. The hill was silent. There were no cicadas. The earth had closed its holes and wouldn't let the ants or the pinacate beetles out. A red wind made the reddish clouds descend until they touched the tips of the sunflowers. A yellow dust rained from the flowers and Don Flor was alone, lying on the patio of his house. There wasn't a single day in sight. The week had run out. Evita and Leli wanted to go back to their house. But the red afternoon spun around them and they stayed there sitting on the burning earth, looking at the Days' abandoned patio and at Don Flor collapsed on the ground, gazing motionless at the sky. Time passed, and Don Flor in his bougainvillea tunic stayed still, laid out in the middle of the patio of his house. The girls stared at him so long that his tunic started to grow huge and the patio very small. Perhaps Our Lord Jesus

Christ was taking their eyes, and that's why all they saw was the ever-larger splotch of the bougainvillea-colored tunic.

"Let's go see Don Flor, he'll tell us."

They went down the hill and around to the front of the house that pulsated white under the red clouds. They knocked at the door and waited. After a while it opened a crack, and then it was flung open wide.

"What sorrows bring you here, little girls?" Don Flor asked them when he appeared in the doorway of his house. They looked at him, tall in his tunic of dark folds, his ears hidden by his black hair.

"We can't see…"

"Come in, come in."

He ushered them into a tiny lilac-painted vestibule. From there, out to the round patio. The bedroom doors led to that patio, and they were all closed. Each door was a different color. The windows looked onto the corral. The house was just like a dovecote. In the center of the patio where there should have been a fountain, Don Flor set out three chairs, had them sit down, and looked at them thoughtfully.

"Well then, so you're the little blonde girls?"

They let themselves be observed in silence.

"Female hair…" said Don Flor, touching their hair with fingers loaded down with rings.

With a quick shove he slid his chair closer to them and leaned over to look into their eyes.

"Male eye," he added.

The girls didn't know what to say; they looked down and stared at the round gray stones.

"There's a lot of water, a lot of water in your eyes."

Don Flor said these words gravely. Then he fell into a distressed silence.

"Between you two and me there is all the water in the world."

When he said this, Don Flor became very sad, rolled his eyes, and clapped loudly several times, as if he were going to shatter the afternoon. Then he put his hands out, palms up in front of him, and fell into a state of rapture. After a while he leaned over Leli, placed a finger between her eyes, and stared at her.

"You are going to go to the other side of the water."

When he took his finger from the girl's forehead, she thought he would leave a hole there. Don Flor shook his hands as if they were wet, turned to look at Eva, and placed his finger on her pale forehead.

"And you…"

He fell silent and seemed puzzled. He took his finger from the girl's forehead and moved it to her knee.

"I will read your knee."

He promptly leaned over the leg that was caked with dirt from the hill, and stayed like that for a long time. Evita didn't move.

"You're not going. You're staying among these days."

"Which ones?" Eva asked fearfully.

"These. Here we are in the center of the days."

His words drank the water of the afternoon and an arid silence fell. The girls felt thirsty as they looked at the dusty patio, through which a hot wind blew. There was not a single plant in the whole house, or the slightest trace of leaves.

"There are no more days… Where did they go?" asked Eva.

"The Week went to the Teloloapan Fair. Only the center of the days is left here," Don Flor replied, looking at them with glassy eyes that smelled of alcohol.

"To the fair?"

"You don't believe me? Come!"

Don Flor stood up and started to walk, swishing the folds of his bougainvillea-colored tunic. The girls watched him walk away. Suddenly he stopped, turned back toward them, and beckoned. They had no choice but to obey and follow this man who was waiting for them impatiently. He stopped in front of a red-painted door.

"See?"

Over the door's red paint, in letters that were a darker red, someone had written SUNDAY, and in smaller letters LUST, and farther down GENEROSITY. The man took a bunch of little black keys from among the folds of his tunic, chose one, and inserted it into the lock on the door. Then he kicked it wide open.

"Come in."

The girls entered behind Don Flor and stood with him in the middle of the room.

"Do you hear?" the man asked in a strange voice.

The girls looked at him in surprise. There was no one in that room with red walls and door, nor was there any sound to be heard.

"You don't hear the whipping?"

The girls looked at his dry, alert eyes, his face tilted toward some sounds that they couldn't hear. Don Flor seemed satisfied, oddly satisfied.

"Listen."

The room held only an incredible smell. They didn't know if it was pleasant or unpleasant. From one of the red walls hung some necklaces made of black shells.

"See? Sunday isn't here. Sunday is at the fair with the other Days."

"No, Sunday isn't here," replied the girls.

Don Flor went over and touched the black shells, then turned back to the girls.

"She's the worst of them all: lustful and wasteful. I haven't been able to fit her with the virtue that would check her vice."

The man shook his head and spun the rings he wore on his fingers. His dry eyes turned back to the girls.

"When it's time for me to visit her, she makes me sweat blood, but I also draw hers. I leave her striped with lashings... Hear her? She's calling me. Listen to her! Hear her cry as she calls to me! She loves pleasure and vices..."

The girls heard nothing. Sunday's room scared them. They looked at Don Flor, whose eyes had grown as dry as the black shells on the necklaces hanging from the wall.

"Listen to her...! Listen...!"

He looked at them again and he was smiling, showing his white teeth.

"I like her skin laid out...it bursts like a guava fruit... Shame of a woman! Shame...! She is flesh for the devil. Shame, from so much beauty!"

"We'll be leaving…" said the girls, frightened.

"What do you mean, leaving? You came here to learn about the Days, and I've only shown you Sunday's lust."

Don Flor burst out laughing. He ran a hand over his black hair and then grew sad.

"Bad day…wicked woman… I hope I don't get lost in her pleasures… I'm afraid of her.

"I hope I don't get lost in her pleasures…!" Don Flor repeated worriedly. When he left Sunday's room, he carefully locked the door.

"I lock it tight so her moans don't escape me. This woman must do penance. As I told you, she makes me sweat blood, but I also draw hers…"

His words fell panting over the girls' blonde heads. They were near the jaws of an unknown animal, with breath as hot as the afternoon. Don Flor stopped at the next door. It was painted pink, and in a darker pink was written SATURDAY, SLOTH, CHASTITY.

"Saturday! Sloth! Chastity!" Don Flor read aloud.

He pushed the door open and they entered a room with pink walls. The floor was covered with cane husks. On the walls were little rag dolls stuck with pins.

"I haven't been able to fit Saturday's virtue onto her, either. She's good for nothing. Nothing!"

Don Flor seemed very displeased. He kicked at the cane husks, and his ring-heavy hand adjusted the pins that threatened to fall out of one of the doll's heads.

"Look at this disrespect! So lazy, she's no good for even a kiss."

Eva and Leli stopped talking to him, not understanding his displeasure. They would have liked to ask him why the dolls were so little and so covered in pins, but instead they kept quiet. They were scared of Don Flor's distraught face.

"I make her scrub and scrub the floor, but she doesn't understand. As soon as I look away, she starts chewing cane and singing while she lies on her mat. I use her by force and without pleasure... She's worthless. But she has to know that I am the master of the Days. The only thing I like is that she doesn't like me..."

Don Flor started to laugh. Laughing, he left the room and locked the door, still amused.

The girls wanted to leave. Every word Don Flor uttered came out of his mouth swollen and smelling of alcohol. Ignoring their wishes, he led them to Friday's room. Beneath that word were written PRIDE and DILIGENCE. The door and the walls were purple. There were kites with long, bright tails hanging from the walls. The room smelled of musk and glycerin.

"You won't find a single word here," explained the man, and he fell silent for a while.

"It's hard to even talk to her. She's a difficult woman, very difficult! I can't even whip her down from her high horse. The punishments the others fear slide right off of her without a word. This woman makes me sad... I can't get her, I just can't get her..."

He seemed truly sad. Preoccupied, he stared at a pile of white baskets in a corner of the room. He shook his head incredulously.

"She's the best weaver among them."

Don Flor touched the white baskets that gave off a fragrance of the countryside, and his eyes grew damp.

"Even if I use her all night long, the easy way or the hard way, I can't get a word out of her. I've left her striped with wounds! But when a woman doesn't want to, she doesn't want to, and a man can break himself on her."

They left Friday's room without speaking. Don Flor's sadness fell over the girls and followed them down the narrow hallway. The room that said THURSDAY was labeled WRATH and MODESTY. Its door and walls were orange like the nopal flower that Don Flor had put in the woman's braid. The room smelled of squash blossoms, and corncobs hung from the ceiling.

"Thursday lives here. She makes the others tremble. I've told her, Woman, you'll end up in hell, turned into a tongue of fire. But she doesn't straighten out. When I whip her, she pounces on me like a cat. Can you believe it? I spend many nights and days in a row with her. She provides many pleasures, many pleasures. But only to me! She's never known another man. I got her nice and young."

Don Flor pounded his chest with pride. The smell that emanated from his tunic made the girls feel sick. He leaned over and picked up the sleeping mat to shake it in front of them.

"See? See?"

The girls didn't see anything. The fingers full of rings pointed to the weave of the mat.

"Don't you see the pleasures? They're drawn right here."

Wednesday's room was green, and the words written in lighter green were ENVY and PATIENCE.

"I haven't been able to fit this one's virtue on her either. Have you seen her?"

"Yes," they said. They had seen Wednesday from afar, wearing her tender green skirt and huipil, her braids full of green ribbons that fell down the back of her neck.

"If she had her way, I would only visit her. That's why I rarely spend the night with her. But she puts up with everything: contempt, beatings, as long as I occasionally let her punish the others."

Don Flor burst out laughing. He turned to look at them with shining eyes in which dry sparks danced.

"She's vicious!"

His laughter reached them smelling of alcohol. They listened to him without understanding.

"Don't get the idea I don't like her. I like her, I like this woman! Not every day. You know there are days for the Days. You should just see how she gets when I offer her the punishments. She's a dog! Have you seen the faces of bitch dogs being mounted? She even drools…!"

Tuesday's room was pale yellow. Her door said AVARICE and ABSTINENCE.

"She's so delicate I don't even like to touch her. She's fragile, and I am strong. I want a body better suited to mine."

Suddenly he seemed to grow furious. His eyes were fixed on the ground and he seemed to be looking for something, then he knelt down and lifted a floor tile. In a hollow in the loose earth, some blue bead earrings were hidden.

"I've told her not to hide anything. I'm going to make her vomit out her lungs, so she can hide them in this hole."

The violence of his words uttered in a low voice made the yellows of the walls start to flicker. Don Flor slammed the door shut behind them. Overcome, he leaned against the hallway wall for a long time before he was calm again. The girls waited, dumbfounded.

Monday's room was blue like her dress. On the door, which was blue as well, the words GLUTTONY and HUMILITY were written in different blues.

"When I touch this one, she licks my hands. Insatiable!"

Don Flor looked at his hands with satisfaction. Then he reached them out, as if expecting the girls to lick them too. His rings were greasy and their colored stones opaque. He stayed like that for a long while, then straightened up and sniffed the air like a dog.

"Smell! Smell!" he urged them.

The girls breathed in sharply, trying to perceive some odor, but none reached them. Monday's room was the only one that didn't smell like anything. The effort they exerted trying to smell made their nausea worsen. Don Flor looked at them and rolled with laughter.

"Can't you smell it? Monday is a glutton for sweets and for men... She turns me into an animal... Sometimes she scares me. Girls, a man with a gluttonous woman beside him is in danger."

He led them to the patio where a round, dry heat awaited them.

"Well then, girls, now you've seen how the Days live,

and what they're like. You've also seen who is master of the Week. And you saw how everything is in disarray: the colors, the sins, the virtues, and the Days. We are in disarray, and that's why I whip the Days, to punish them for their faults."

Don Flor fell silent. In the patio's heat, the girls saw that his tunic was dirty, and that the fingers he turned his rings around were all coated in grime. The patio smelled sour, and the words emerged broken from the man's mouth. Don Flor loomed over them and gazed at them with his dry, black eyes. Inside them were bloody lakes and dark stones.

"Tell me, little girls, what is your sorrow?"

The girls had forgotten their fears. They saw Don Flor's eyes and smelled the waves of scents that wafted out from cracks under the colored doors, merging in the center of the patio and forming a whirlwind of vapors. Our Lord Jesus Christ had not punished them, and the only thing they wanted was to go back to their own house, where the walls and the garden smelled like walls and garden.

"People around here treat me badly, little girls. You two are the first ones to come and visit me. People come from Mexico City, though, in search of solace from their sorrows. They're frightened when they come to me, and I show them the disarray of the Days and the disarray of man. They come here to ask me to punish the day when their fate will be decided. They want to get a head start and go into it with the day already tired. There are those who are running for office, and I punish the day of elections. Women come as well, to ask for punishment for the day of their rivals. They all leave me a good payment and go away content, after watching me punish the Day of their choosing. When they see the Day bleed, they start to take out their money…"

Don Flor waited a while and started to laugh. The girls didn't know what to say and stared resolutely at the ground. The man leaned over their heads and asked, "And you, little girls, what punishment do you want?"

The girls looked at each other in fear; they wanted to go home and be near Philip II and Candelaria. Don Flor and his round house scared them.

"I am the master of the Days. I am the Century. Tell me what day you were offended, and you'll see what we do to whichever Day you want."

The girls looked Don Flor in the eyes.

"Come back, it doesn't matter that there is so much water between you two and me. I'll do you the favor anyway. The days are the same for everyone! You want to whip Thursday? Tell me, which Day do you want to see bleed?"

They looked back down at the ground. They didn't want to see the man's eyes or hear his dire words.

"Tell me, little girls, what Day do you want to see bleed?" Don Flor repeated the same question over and over.

"Which Day do you want to see bleed?"

His voice didn't change and he didn't lose patience at their silence.

"Which Day do you want to see bleed?"

It was a long time before they could reach the door. They didn't notice whether they left it open or closed. All they wanted was to reach their house. When they went in through the hallway, past an astonished Rutilio, the voice repeated, "Which Day do you want to see bleed? Which one, little girls? Which one? Tell me which Day you want to see bleed."

They started to cry. Their father explained that the Days were white, and that the only week was Holy Week: Palm Sunday, Holy Monday, Holy Tuesday, Holy Wednesday, Holy Thursday, Good Friday, Holy Saturday, and Easter Sunday. But it was hard to forget the Week of Colors locked up in Don Flor's house.

"Which Day do you need to see bleed? Which one? Which one?"

"You two are like crazy birds, hopping from Holy Week to the Week of Colors locked in Don Flor's house," Candelaria told them when she drew the mosquito net, which did nothing to protect them from Don Flor's question. "Which Day do you need to see bleed? Which one?"

In the morning, Candelaria didn't bring them breakfast. Rutilio served them their oatmeal and milk. He looked at them fearfully. Their father and mother had gone out to run an errand.

"So they don't bother you two," Rutilio explained. The girls looked at him in fear as well.

"Are you sure he talked to you?" Rutilio asked, handing them the little basket of cakes.

"Who?"

"Don Flor."

From the white morning spread over the tablecloth, the question arose: "Which Day do you need to see bleed?

Which one, little girls?"

"Yes…he talked a lot…" and they started to cry.

"Did you leave the door open?" asked Rutilio.

"I don't know…" Evita replied.

"Yes, yes…" Leli said.

"That's what they're saying, that you two were the ones who left the door open. There was such a stench coming from the place that the mule drivers noticed when they passed by, and they went in to the patio and found him lying there right in the center. They say it was the women who killed him, because the Week disappeared… Are you sure he talked to you…? They're saying he'd been dead for several days…"

THE DAY WE WERE DOGS

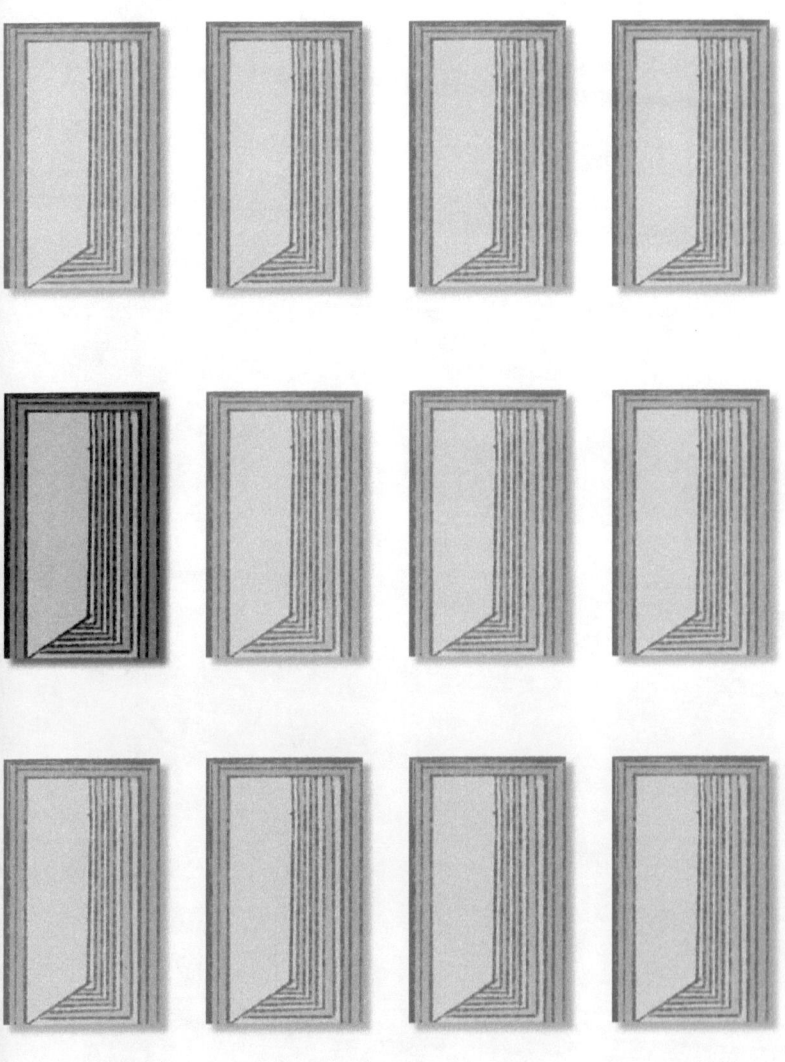

The day we were dogs wasn't just any day, thought it started the same as usual. We woke up at six in the morning, but then we realized it was a day with two days inside it. Eva opened her eyes lying face up, and without moving from her position, she looked at one day and then at the other. I'd opened my own eyes some time before, and to avoid seeing the immensity of the empty house, I'd been looking at her. Why hadn't we gone to Mexico City? I still don't know. We asked to stay home, and no one opposed our wish. The night before, the courtyard had filled with suitcases: everyone was fleeing the August heat. The suitcases had departed in a horse-drawn carriage very early in the morning; the table held half-finished cups of milky coffee and plates with lumpy oatmeal. Words of advice and recommendation were strewn over the courtyard tiles. Eva and I looked at them disdainfully. We were masters of the patios, the gardens, and the bedrooms. When we took possession of the house, a great weight fell upon us. What could we do with the archways, the windows, doors, and furniture? The day turned solid, the violet sky grew heavy with dark paper, and fear settled over the pillars and plants. We wandered silently through the house and watched our hair turn to tatters. We didn't have anything to do, or anyone to ask what we should do. In the kitchen, the servants huddled around the stove to eat and doze off. The beds weren't made, and no one watered the ferns or cleared the dirty mugs from the dining table. When it grew dark, the servants' songs reached us heavy with crimes and sorrows, and the house sank that day like a stone falling off a very steep cliff.

We woke up resolved not to repeat the previous day. The new day shone double and untouched. Eva looked at the two parallel days that glittered like two lines drawn on the water. Then she looked at the wall, at Christ in his white robes. Next her eyes moved to the other picture, an image of Buddha wrapped in his orange robes, thoughtful in a yellowy landscape. Between the two portraits that kept watch over the head of her bed, Eva had placed a newspaper clipping with a photograph of a woman in a beret aboard a boat. KRUPSKAYA ON THE NEVA, said the caption under the photograph.

"I like the Russians," said Eva, and then she clapped to call the servants. No one responded to her summons. We looked at each other without surprise. Eva was clapping from one of the days, and her claps didn't reach the day of the kitchen.

"Let's go nose around," she said.

And she jumped over to my bed to look at me up close. Her blonde hair fell over her forehead. From my bed she jumped to the ground, then put a finger over her lips and carefully moved into the day that was progressing in parallel to the other. I followed her. No one around. That day was alone, and just as scary as the other. The still trees, the round sky, green like a tender meadow, and no one there, either, no horse, no rider, just abandoned. The August heat that had caused the escape to Mexico City emanated from the well. Toni was lying beside a tree, attached to his chain. He watched us attentively, and we saw that he was in our day.

"Toni is good," said Eva, and she petted his open mouth.

Then she lay down beside him, and I lay on his other side.

"Did you have breakfast, Toni?"

Toni didn't answer, just looked at us sadly. Eva got up and disappeared among the plants. She came running back and flopped back down beside Toni.

"I told them to make food for three dogs and no people."

I didn't ask any questions. Once we were next to Toni, the house lost weight. Ants walked over the day's ground; an earthworm peeked out of a hole, and when I touched it with a fingertip, it turned into a red ring. There were pieces of leaves, bits of branches, tiny rocks, and the black earth smelled like magnolia perfume. The other day was off to the side. Toni, Eva, and I looked fearlessly at its gigantic towers and its fixed, purple-colored winds.

"So, what's your name going to be? Think about your dog name, I'm trying to come up with mine."

"I'm a dog?"

"Yeah, we're dogs."

I agreed and moved closer to Toni, who turned his head

in annoyance. I remembered that he wouldn't go to heaven; now I would have the same fate as him. "Animals don't go to heaven." Our Lord Jesus Christ had not set up a place for dogs in heaven. Lord Buddha hadn't set up a place in Nirvana for dogs, either. In our house, it was very important to be good so we would go to heaven. We couldn't save money, or kill animals; we were vegetarian, and on Sundays we tossed our allowance off the balcony for someone to pick up, so we would learn not to hoard anything. We lived day to day. People in town came sniffing around the balconies of our house: "They're Spanish," they said, looking sidelong at us. We hadn't known we weren't from there, because right there was where we were earning our place in heaven, whichever of the two: the white-and-blue one or the orange-and-yellow one. Now neither of them had room for the three of us. The alchemists, the Greeks, the anarchists, the Romantics, the occultists, the Franciscans, and the Romans all filled shelves in the library and conversations at the table. They had a place separate from the Evangelicals, the Vedas, and the poets. For dogs, there was no other place besides the foot of the tree. And afterward? Afterward we'd be tossed into any old field.

"I've got my name."

"Yeah?" Eva's head rose up.

"Yeah: Christ."

Eva looked at me enviously.

"Christ? That's a good name for a dog."

Eva settled her head back down on her front paws and closed her eyes.

"I've got mine, too," she said, suddenly straightening up.

"What is it?"

"Buddha!"

"That's a very good name for a dog."

And Buddha stretched out beside Toni and grunted with pleasure.

No one came to visit in Toni, Christ, and Buddha's day. The house was far away, off in its other day. The church clocktower's bells did not chime anything. The ground started to grow very hot: the earthworms went into their holes, the pinacate beetles looked for damp places under the rocks, and the ants cut up acacia leaves, which they used as green parasols. There was thirst in the place the dogs were. Buddha barked impatiently to ask for water, Toni did the same, and then Christ joined in the barking. Along a distant path came Rutilio's feet in huarache sandals. He was carrying three bowls of water. Indifferently, he set one bowl in front of Toni, looked at Christ and Buddha, and placed a bowl in front of each of their snouts. Rutilio patted the dogs' heads and they wagged their tails in thanks. It was hard to drink water with their tongues. Later, the old servant brought lunch in a pot and spooned it into a large dish. The dogs' rice had bones and meat. Christ and Buddha looked at each other, astonished: Dogs weren't vegetarian? Toni raised his upper lip, growled ferociously through his white fangs, and snatched up the pieces of meat. Christ and Buddha stuck their noses into the dish and ate the rice that was wet as paste. Toni finished his food and drowsily watched his companions eating with their tongues. Then they lay on their front paws, too. The sun burned, the ground burned, and the dog food weighed them down like a bag of rocks. They fell asleep in their day, separate from the day of the house. They were awakened by a rocket that came from the other day. A great silence followed. Alert, they listened to the other afternoon. Another rocket exploded, and the three dogs started running toward the sound. Toni had to stop running, because the chain kept him by the tree. Christ and Buddha jumped over the shrubs and headed toward the front gate.

"Where are you little brats going?" Rutilio shouted from the other day.

The dogs reached the entranceway; it was hard to open the front gate, since the latches were high up. Finally, they emerged into the street lit by the four o'clock sun; it shone radiant as a still image. The stones gleamed in the dust. No one was there. No one except for two men bathed in blood, embracing in their struggle. Buddha sat down on the curb and looked at them with wide eyes. Christ settled in very close to Buddha and gawked at them as well. The men were hurling accusations at one another in the other day: "I'll show you…!" "Ohhh! Son of a bitch…!" Their muffled voices came from very far away. One man blocked the hand that held the gun, and with his free hand stamped the other's chest with his knife. He was holding on to the other man's body, and, as if his strength were giving out, he slid to the ground in that embrace. The man with the gun held firm, on his feet in the radiant afternoon. His white shirt and pants were turning red with blood. In a single movement he freed his hand and put the gun to the middle of his kneeling enemy's forehead. A sharp sound split the other afternoon in two, and opened a hole in the kneeling man's head. The man fell face up and stared at the sky.

"Bastard!" cried the man standing on the stones, while his legs continued to rain blood. Then he also raised his eyes to look up at the same sky, and after a while he turned toward the dogs, who, sitting on the curb two meters away, were staring openmouthed.

Everything went quiet. The other afternoon rose so high that, down below, the street was left outside of it. In the distance, several men with rifles appeared. They approached as all men do, in white, with their hats in their hands. They walked slowly. The pounding of their huaraches resonated from very far away. In the street, there were no trees to muffle the sound of their steps; only white walls, off which the footsteps echoed ever closer, like a drumroll on a feast day. The uproar suddenly stopped when they reached the hurt man.

"Did you kill him?"

"I did, just ask those girls."

The men looked at the dogs.

"Did you two see it?"

"Woof! Woof!" Buddha replied.

"Woof! Woof!" Christ replied.

"Arrest him, then."

They took the man away, and the only remaining trace of him was the blood on the stones in the street. It was writing his ending, and the dogs read his bloody fate and turned to look at the dead man.

Some time passed, the front gate of the house was still open, and the dogs were transfixed, sitting on the curb, still staring at the dead man. A fly landed on the wound on his forehead, then rubbed its feet together and moved to the hair. After a moment it returned to the forehead, looked at the wound, and rubbed its feet again. Just when the fly went back to the wound, a woman came and threw herself on the dead man. But he didn't care about the fly or the woman. Stone-faced, he kept staring at the sky. Other people came and leaned over to look at his eyes. It started to grow dark, and Buddha and Christ were still there, not moving or barking. They looked like two street dogs, and no one paid them any mind.

"Eva! Leli!" the shout came from high above. The dogs jumped.

"You just wait till your parents get home! I'll show you!"

Rutilio led them into the house. He put a chair in the courtyard, very near the wall, and sat down solemnly to look at the dogs, who, lying at his feet, looked up at him attentively. Candelaria brought over a lamp and sashayed back to the kitchen. Soon after, song flooded the house with sadness.

"It's your fault I can't go sing…! Bad girls!" complained Rutilio.

Christ and Buddha heard him all the way from the other day. Rutilio, his chair, the lamp, and the dead man, they were all in the parallel day, separated from theirs by an invisible line.

"You just wait, the witches are going to come and drink your blood. People say they love the blood of blondes. I'm going to tell Candelaria to leave the embers burning so they can warm their legs. Then, they'll go from the stove to your beds and have their fill. That's what you deserve, for being wicked!"

The fire with its burning embers, Candelaria, Rutilio, the songs, and the witches all passed before the dogs' eyes like shapes projected onto a separate time. Rutilio's words circulated through the house's endless courtyard and did not touch them. On the floor of the day of the dogs, wood lice were going to sleep. The wood lice's tiredness was contagious, and Christ and Buddha, curled up on their front paws, nodded off.

"Come to dinner!"

They were seated on the kitchen floor, in the circle of servants drinking alcohol, and given a plate of beans with sausage. The dogs were falling over from exhaustion. Until yesterday, they had still dined on oatmeal with milk, and the taste of sausage made them nauseous.

"Carry them to bed, it's like they're drunk!"

They were placed in the same bed, the lamp was extinguished, and the servants left. The dogs slept in the other day, at the foot of the tree, with the chain around their necks, near the green-parasoled ants and the red earthworms. After a while they were startled awake. The parallel day was there, sitting in the middle of the room. The walls breathed burning embers; witches were peering in through the cracks at the blue veins in their temples. It was all very dark. In one of the beds lay the dead man with the open head; beside him, standing, the stamped man streamed blood. Very far away, in the depths of the garden, the servants slept; Mexico City, with their parents and siblings—who knows where that was. The other day, however, was right there, very close to them, without any barking at all, with its still-image dead, in the stilled afternoon, with the giant fly that landed on the giant wound and cleaned its feet. In our sleep, without our noticing, we passed from one day into the other and lost the day we were dogs.

"Don't be scared, we're dogs…" I said.

But Eva knew that was no longer true. We had discovered that man's heaven was not the same as dog heaven.

Dogs didn't share in our crime and bloodshed.

Before the Trojan war I had the days at my fingertips, and I walked through them easily. The sky was tangible. Nothing was out of my reach, and I was part of this world. Eva and I were one.

"I'm hungry," Eva said.

And the two of us ate the same mash, slept at the same time, and dreamed an identical dream. At night I heard the wind come down from Canyon de la Mano. It made its way along the stone crests of the mountains, blew hotly over the crests of the iguanas, descended into town, frightened the coyotes, entered the corrals, burned the red jacaranda flowers, and split the papaya trees in the garden.

"It's on the roof."

Eva's voice was mine. We heard the roof tiles move. Scorpions tumbled from the ceiling beams and the crystalline geckos broke their little pink feet when they hit the floor tiles of my room. Protected by my mosquito net I touched Eva's heart, which ran through the plains of my own, fleeing the gusts that blew from Canyon de la Mano. The wind did not burn us.

"Were you two scared last night?"

"No. We like the wind."

Afterward, the house was in disarray. With her braids undone, Candelaria served us our oats.

"This wicked wind! We should tie its hair to a rock, so it'll leave us in peace!"

"It's the hot rage of crazy women," added Rutilio.

"That's why I say we should fix its mop to the rocks and let it howl from there."

Candelaria had a lot of rage. Eva and I moved around intact within her voice, and in the garden, we looked at the demolished flowers.

"It was back before Leli was born..." my mother sometimes said.

Those words were the only terrible thing that happened to me before the Trojan War. Every time that "before Leli was born" was uttered, the wind, the heliotropes, and the words moved further away from me. I entered a shapeless world where there was only vapor, where I myself was a shapeless vapor. Eva's slightest gesture returned me to the center of things, set order to the jumbled house, and the blurry figures of my parents recovered their impenetrable enigma.

"Let's see what the lady is doing..."

The lady's name was Elisa and she was my mother. In the afternoons, Elisa would hide away in her room, go over to the dressing table, and close the mirror doors. She didn't open them again until night, when it was time to put powders on her face. When she lay down on the bed, her blonde braid divided her back into two.

"Who's there?"

"No one."

"What do you mean, no one?"

"It's Leli," replied Eva.

Elisa hid something and then sat up. Through the mosquito net, her face and body looked like a photograph.

"Get out of my room!"

We went back to the courtyard gallery to walk it up and down, down and up, from stone to stone, not stepping on the cracks, and repeating "fountain, fountain," or any other word, until from so much repetition it became a noise that did not mean *fountain*. At that point we would switch to a different word, astonished, searching for one that wouldn't come undone. When Elisa threw us out of her room, we repeated her name on every stone and asked, "Why is she named Elisa?" and we were stunned by the secret reasons for names. And Antonio? It was very mysterious that her husband should be named Antonio. Elisa-Antonio, Antonio-Elisa, Elisa-Antonio, Antonio, Elisa, and the two names repeated became only one, and then none. Confounded, we sat down in the middle of the afternoon. The orange sky stretched over the treetops; the clouds wafted down to the water in the fountain and in the sink where Estefanía was washing sheets and the master's shirts. Antonio had green and yellow sparks in his eyes. If we looked at them up close, it was as if we were within a grove in the garden.

"Look, Antonio, I'm inside your eyes!"

"Yes, that's why I drew you just how I wanted," he replied on Sundays, when he trimmed our bangs.

Antonio was my father, and he didn't send us to the hair salon because "little girls' necks must be soft, and the hairdresser might shave them with a razor." It was a shame not to go to the salon. Adrián spun among his colored jars, sharpening razors and brandishing scissors in the air. He chatted as if he were trimming words, and he was trailed by a violent perfume.

"Yep! The little blondes want me bad, but their dad won't pay for a hairdresser."

Sitting in the round afternoon, we'd remember our visits to Adrián, and also to Mendiola, who sold "kisses" wrapped in yellow paper.

"Here's the little pair of canaries!"

Mendiola put a kiss in each of our hands. We both liked visiting. When we went to the movies, we saw the two friends from afar. We couldn't talk to them, or to Don Amparo, the candle seller, because we were sitting between Elisa and Antonio, who only greeted people with a nod of the head. They liked silence, and when we talked, they'd say, "Read! Be virtuous!"

We peered at the gods drawn in the books, and we found virtue there. The Greek gods were the most handsome. Apollo was gold and Aphrodite, silver. In India, the gods had many arms and hands.

"They must be very good thieves."

Do not let your left hand know what your right hand is

doing. We would steal fruit with our left hands. What about the Indian gods? They had a left hand, a right hand, an upper and a lower hand, a friendly hand and a mean hand, and a hand in between. Impossible to tell which was the one that shouldn't know what the others were doing.

"Oh, if we were like them, we would steal everything: screws, sweets, flags, all at the same time!"

The other gods were like us. Even Our Lord Jesus Christ had only two hands nailed to the cross. Huitzilopochtli was a dark little lump with hands and no arms, but he scared us so much we preferred not to look at him, motionless on one of the bookshelves.

"What would a cross for Kali be like?"

"Like a windmill."

"A cross, I'm saying, not a windmill."

"A cross…? Like a cross."

"You'd have to nail one hand on top of another and another, with a nail as long as a sword."

"What about the middle hand?"

"We'd leave it loose like a tail, to shoo away flies."

"We can't. We'd have to nail it, too."

"On the left or on the right?"

"Let's go ask Elisa."

"What do you want?" Elisa asked in her photograph voice.

"Nothing."

"Then get out of my room!" And she hid something again.

We went out into the courtyard with the shame of knowing that Elisa was hiding something in her bed. We hopped along the flagstones repeating her name, and when only the noise remained, we went back to her room.

"What do you want?"

"Your husband is calling you…he's in the chicken coop."

The chicken coop was not a place for Antonio, and Elisa looked at us curiously. But the chicken coop was back behind the corrals, and it would take Elisa a good while to go there and return to her bed. She left. Her bed was hot and a vapor of perfume rose from the pillows. We searched for what she was hiding.

"Look!"

Eva showed me a little bag of kisses and candied fruit. We took two kisses and ate them.

"Look!"

A dry leaf marked the pages of the book Elisa kept under her pillow.

"Let's go!"

We hurried off, without the sweets and with the book. We looked for a safe place to page through it. All places were dangerous. We looked at the treetops and chose the greenest, the highest. Sitting on a forked branch, we read *The Iliad*. Thus began the ill-fated Trojan War.

"Sing, oh muse, of the rage of Achilles!"

Elisa's rage lasted many weeks. We, deafened by the roar of battle, hardly had time to listen to her.

"Where do they hide all day?"

"Hm… Who knows…"

Up above, among the leaves, waited Nestor, Odysseus, Achilles, Agamemnon, Hector, Andromache, Paris, and

Helen. Without our noticing, the days started to grow separate from one another. Then the days were severed from the nights; then the wind detached from Canyon de la Mano and blew foreignly over the trees, the sky grew distant from the garden, and we found ourselves in a divided and dangerous world.

"Don't let the dogs devour my flesh," said Hector from the ground, raising his arm in supplication. Achilles, standing, his foot resting on the fallen man's throat, looked at him in contempt.

"Poor Hector!"

"I'm on Achilles's side," said Eva, suddenly unfamiliar.

And she looked at me. She had never looked at me before. I looked at her. She was straddling the tree branch like another person who wasn't me. I was startled by her hair, her voice, and her eyes. She was another. I felt dizzy. The tree moved away from me and the ground plummeted. She also didn't recognize my voice, my hair, or my eyes. And she also felt dizzy. We climbed down, clutching the trunk in fear that it would vanish.

"I'm on Hector's side," I repeated back on the ground, feeling like it was no longer earth beneath my feet. I looked at the house, and its twisted roofs were alien to me. I went to the kitchen, sure that I would find it just as before, just like me, but the wooden door admitted me with hostility. The maids had changed. Their eyes glittered separate from their hair. They chopped onions with movements that seemed ferocious. The knife sound was separate from the onion smell.

"I'm with Achilles," Eva repeated, hugging Estefanía's pink skirts.

"I'm with Hector," I said firmly, hugging Candelaria's lilac skirts.

And with Hector I started to learn about the world on my own. The world, on my own, was only sensations. I split off from my steps and heard them echo all by their lonesome in the courtyard. My chest hurt. The smell of vanilla was no longer vanilla, it was vibrations. The wind of Canyon de la Mano split off from Candelaria's voice. I didn't touch anything; I was out of the world. I sought out my father and mother because I was terrified of the idea of being alone. The house was also alone, and it echoed like stones we throw in a solitary field. My parents didn't know, and words were useless, because they had also emptied of their contents. At dusk, separated from the afternoon, I went into the kitchen.

"Candelaria, do you love me very much?"

"Who could love such a bad little blonde?"

Candelaria started to laugh. Her laughter rang out in another instant. Night fell like a black bell. Above her was Glory, but I didn't see it. Hector and Achilles roamed the Shadow Kingdom, and Eva and I followed them, stepping on black holes.

"Leli, do you love me?"

"Yes, I love you very much."

Now we loved each other. It was very strange to love someone, to love everyone: Elisa, Candelaria, Rutilio. We loved them because we could not touch them.

Eva and I looked at our hands, feet, hair, so enclosed

in themselves, so far away from us. It was incredible that my hand was me, since it moved as if it were its own self. And we loved our hands, too, the way we did other people, for they were as strange as us or as unreal as the trees, the patios, the kitchen. We were losing corporeality, just as the world had lost corporeality. That's why we loved each other, with the desperate love of ghosts. And there was no solution. Before the Trojan War we were two in one, we didn't love, we just were, without really knowing where. Hector and Achilles did not stay with us. They just left us alone, circling, circling us, not touching us or touching anything ever again. They, too, spun in the Shadow Kingdom, unable to get used to their condition as lost souls. At night, I heard Hector dragging his weapons. Eva heard Achilles's footsteps and the metallic hiss of his shield.

"I'm with Hector," I declared in the morning, between the evanescent walls of my room.

"I'm with Achilles," said Eva's voice, far away from her tongue. Both voices were very far away from the bodies sitting there on the same bed.

THE TIZTLA THEFT

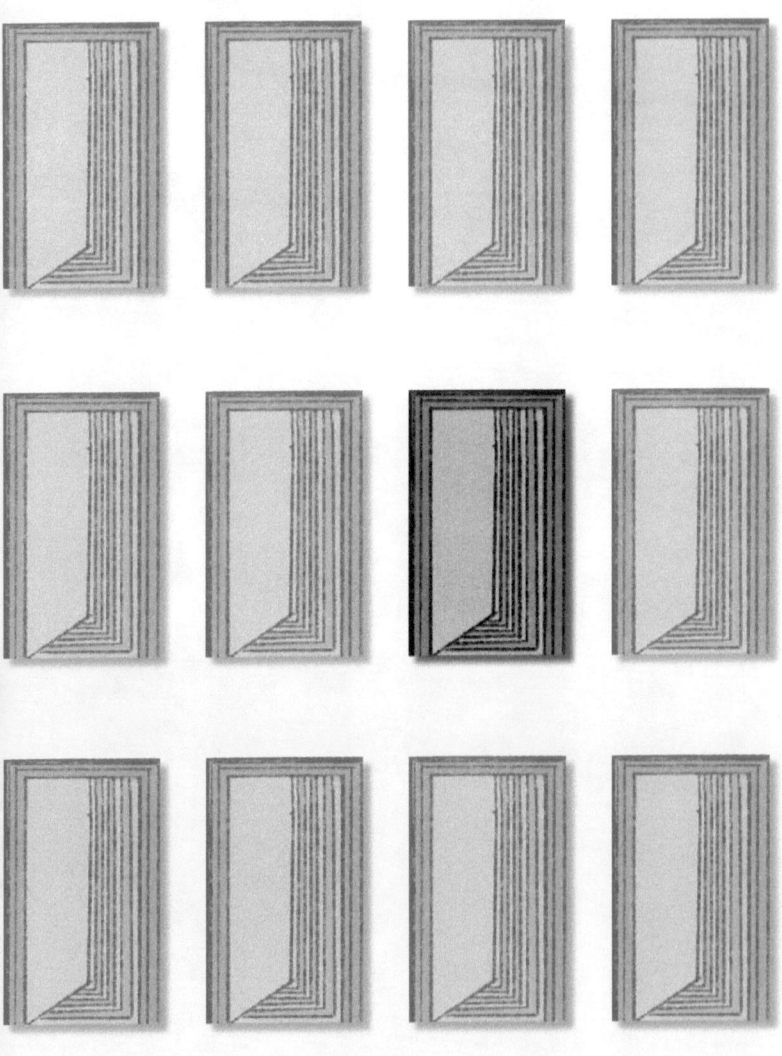

Tiztla is a small town located in the south of the Republic of Mexico. Its inhabitants are small and silent. Its nights are deep, and when the sun sets, man is afraid. The summer months are as hot and dry as the heart of a stone set out in the sun. People go through life drowsy and hot-headed. Fire courses under the earth, and the gardens boil with the song of cicadas and crickets. A constant "aw! ay! aw!" ignites the imagination. The fields fill with demons, and on occasion they breach the town to enter men's eyes. People sleep alert in their hammocks. The incessant murmur lulls them, while evil, in the form of scoundrels and blades, spies on them. They sleep hearing many things that people in the capital have never heard. Leaning always beside them, their machetes.

It was summer when the break-in happened, and the women saw something in the shining light that the men did not see. That's why, the morning after the theft, the authorities were merciless with the maids and forgot the men of the house.

"These women know!" insisted the police chief.

"Of course they know!" his underlings replied.

"Just tell me what you saw."

And the police chief turned his glassy eyes on Fili, as if he wanted to yank some hidden image out of the woman's pupils. Fili lowered her eyelids defensively.

"Well look, sir, I saw fifty men..."

"Fifty men!"

"Yes, sir, fifty white men with embers for eyes, and they were walking real quiet in the garden. Each of them carried a torch in his hand and...they were dancing..."

"Dancing? Write this down, deputy! Fifty white men, dancing in the garden, with torches in their hands."

The deputy scribbled.

"And after the dance, what did they do?" the chief asked sternly.

"After the dance...? Well, nothing, they danced and danced all night long..."

"Write, deputy, that the fifty men kept on dancing."

The police chief seemed disconcerted. He kept his glassy eyes on Fili as she lowered her head, squinted, and smoothed her braids over her chest. The chief looked around and made a kind of grimace, which was his attempt at a smile, toward the lady of the house and her daughters. They were listening to the interrogation with a distracted air, as if they weren't the least bit interested. Now it was the turn of Carmen, the cook.

"Oh, sir, I saw lots of men, lots of men!"

"How many?" asked the police chief.

"I counted thirty-seven."

"Only thirty-seven?" cried the chief, disappointed.

"It's just that I can't count any higher. I learned up to thirty-seven...but there were a lot more. Each of them had a machete in his hand...and what machetes they were, sir, they shimmered! They shone in the night like white fire. And the men were all crouched over, crouched over..."

"Take note, deputy: over thirty-seven crouching men, with shining machetes in their hands."

The deputy nervously took note.

"And what else did you see?" the police chief asked, his voice severe.

Carmen stared at him, hesitant.

"Well, I saw...I saw the plants bend over, too, as the men went by, and they surrounded the plants, surrounded them..."

"Did you write down what the witness said?"

"Yes, sir, the plants bent over as the crouching criminals surrounded them," the deputy declared.

"Do you have anything to add to your statement?"

"Me? Nothing. That was all I saw, sir."

And Carmen took a step back, looking out of the corner of her eye at Fili, who had listened closely to her words.

"And you! What did you see?"

Candelaria, the washerwoman, her hands pink from the soap and water, took a step forward and prepared to speak seriously.

"You see, sir, I am a sound sleeper, and I was very lost in my dreams when Carmen woke me up. There's someone in the garden, she said. Stop that nonsense, I replied, and turned over. Yes, someone is out in the garden, Fili said, and she was trembling something awful. Then I shook off my sleep and looked out the window, and I saw what they saw."

"Be specific about what you saw."

"Well, I *was* specific, I saw what they saw," replied Candelaria, annoyed by the man's curtness.

"But what was it that they saw?"

"Why do I have to repeat it? I have a lot to do and I can't be wasting my time on words. I've always said so much tongue-flapping doesn't do any good. A body can talk and talk, and the sun rises and sets, and the moon comes out, and the chores are still undone..."

"That's true, but these are extraordinary circumstances. Please do me the favor of saying what you saw, or you will be arrested as an accessory after the fact," said the police chief, shooting the lady of the house a complicit glance. His look was unreciprocated, since the lady was busy staring at the tulips lying on the ground.

"They're right when they say the higher you rise, the more you earn for doing nothing," replied an angry Candelaria.

"Enough back talk! Say what you saw."

"Well, what else could I have seen: a bunch of men with their matching knives..."

"Write this down: while the witness slept, a bunch of men armed with knives invaded the garden..."

"Is that all?" asked Candelaria, preparing to walk away.

"And where were these men headed?"

"Only God knows that... They were there, who can say

what their intentions were…"

"The witness does not know the intruders' intentions," dictated the police chief. Then, smiling, he turned to the lady of the house.

"And you, ma'am, could you please tell me what you heard, what you saw, etc.?"

The lady of the house opened her eyes wide and thought for some minutes. The chorus of onlookers fell silent.

"I heard the dog barking angrily. I got a chair, climbed onto it, and looked through the window of the door into the courtyard, and then I saw some men at the back of the garden. Some of them carried torches in their hands…others, machetes…others, I think, had nothing…"

"Write this down, deputy! Make note of the dog's sudden appearance!"

"It wasn't sudden, he had been barking for half an hour," the lady corrected him.

"Sudden in the statements. It's the first time the dog has been mentioned, in this statement," the police chief politely replied.

The spectators looked at each other and made signs of admiration regarding the authority's wisdom. The chief turned back to the lady.

"And how many men were there?"

"Oh, I didn't count. But…how many could there be? Maybe fourteen…? Thirty-two? No. Maybe seven…I don't know, they moved around a lot, you know…?"

"Between seven and thirty-two criminals," the chief dictated.

"I can't say the exact number, but it was approximately that, between seven and thirty-two," the lady repeated distractedly.

"Let us move on now to a visual inspection," said the police chief in a pompous voice.

The chief, followed by the lady, the children, the servants, and the onlookers who had entered the house, all headed to the back of the garden. The trees displayed deep machete gashes; the bananas were on the ground; the tulips were hacked to bits; and the ferns, like hair spread over the ground, were drying out slowly in the sun. The criminals hated plants. It was as if they had entered the house to put an end to the greenery in the garden.

"Take note, deputy!"

The deputy took note, while the police and peasants who had entered the house gazed indifferently at the destruction.

"On to the storeroom," said the lady of the house.

She led the group to a room built atop the wall that separated the garden from the street. The storeroom was enormous, with a low roof and a brick floor. It had no windows, and only a small, permanganate-painted door led into that inhospitable space. It had been only three years since Don Antonio, the master of the house, had ordered it built. No one knew why he had built it. The limescale on the damp-stained walls, the room's gigantic size, and the absence of light all lent the place a mysterious, empty look. Words sounded hollow in there, and its cold, viscous silence would clog up a person's nose.

The chief and his companions entered in silence.

Something, there inside, made them hold their breath. This was precisely where the criminals' steps had led. The walls were full of holes, the bricks pried up here and there, and some sacks of corn had been hacked to pieces, spilling grains that shone warm and golden in the dampness. The mess of bricks and trampled corn imposed silence. The police chief was perplexed.

"Take note of this act of villainy, deputy," he said, to give himself time to think of something more appropriate to say.

His words were the cue for everyone else to start talking at the same time.

"Holy Christ!"

"Praise God!"

"Lord save us!"

"The Devil's been here!"

"These degenerates came in the Demon's name!"

"Yes, they were here all night long," said Candelaria.

"Oh, it was already sunup when they left," Carmen chimed in.

"The strangest thing is that they didn't take anything," the lady explained to the police chief, who listened to her in astonishment. The others readied themselves to hear the tale they already knew by heart, because since seven that morning in Tiztla, no one had spoken of anything else.

"Before going to sleep I checked the whole house. As you know, my husband has been in Mexico City for the past three days. When I woke up, I thought something was happening...and it scared me. After I saw the men through the window, I woke the children and told them to be quiet, since the men could come into the bedrooms and kill us if they realized we were spying on them. The children were very brave, especially this little girl here. Just imagine, she wanted to get up on the chair to see for herself what was happening!"

The lady reached out a hand and placed it on Eva's head. The girl turned red and looked down to avoid the chief's look of admiration.

"Would you allow me, ma'am, to question the girl as well? It's just a formality."

"Of course, ask her whatever you like!" the lady conceded.

"Well now, Eva dear, what did you see in the garden?"

The girl was silent.

"What did you see, sweetheart? It's okay, nothing will happen to you," the man insisted when the girl's obstinate eyes met his.

"Well, I saw some men who were burning the garden. There were lots of them, lots and lots. I think they were happy... And I also saw..." Eva snapped her mouth shut. The police chief waited, leaning over her, but the girl hid her face.

"What else did you see, sweetheart?" he asked solicitously.

The girl bit her lip and stared stubbornly at the ground.

"Tell us what else you saw!" her mother ordered.

"Nothing..." Eva replied.

"Tell us what you saw, dear," the man insisted in a sugarcoated voice.

"Nothing!" the girl answered firmly.

"Are you going to say what you saw or not?" her mother shouted, shaking her.

"No!" the girl said.

"Don't frighten her, ma'am. If she's scared, she'll never talk. What did you see, sweetheart?" the chief asked once again. Evita heard more rage than kindness in his honeyed voice.

"Tell me now, what did those little eyes of yours see?"

The girl looked at him resentfully.

"Don't scare her! Let her talk," cried one of the onlookers.

"Speak! What did you see?" her mother shouted indignantly, consumed by curiosity.

"Nothing!"

"She saw something! She saw something! But she's not going to say it, she's afraid," the neighbors said.

"Yes, she did see something," agreed the chief, looking at the girl hopelessly.

If Eva saw something, no one ever knew. She was determined to keep quiet, and the others hung upon her words to no avail. Exasperated by her attitude, they decided to keep quiet too, and they turned silently toward the wall that the criminals had breached in order to enter. The wall was quite high and thick; the robbers had made a hole very near the ground. The chief crawled into it and emerged easily into the street. Astonished, he went back inside.

"So, they entered this way," he said, deep in thought.

"Yes, sir, this way," Eva said calmly.

"And how do you know, honey?" the man asked with hatred.

Little Eva fell silent again. The chief turned his back on her, feigning indifference. Annoyed by the child's gaze, he tried to reconstruct the events.

"First, they bored through the wall; then they came in through the hole and headed to the storeroom, where they broke down the door, destroyed the sacks of corn, the floor, and the walls; then they went out into the yard to cause more damage, and they hacked the plants to bits. Is that all, ma'am?"

"Yes, sir. How odd that they didn't steal a thing," the lady of the house said again.

"It's theft with no theft. Very strange, ma'am."

"Very strange. Look, they didn't even take the clothes that were out."

That area of the garden was where Candelaria hung clothes out to dry. The night before, she had left them hanging, and there all the garments still were, white and fresh.

"Untouched! They didn't even take the sheets. Did you see, deputy?"

The scribe nodded.

"Well, write it down! Don't wait for me to dictate everything. These people are numbskulls," he added, turning to the lady. "These people" hung his head.

The chief seemed to think he had observed enough and approached the lady.

"May I speak to you in private?"

The lady looked at him in consternation, unsure what he wanted from her, and nodded. The two of them retired to a spot a little ways off. The chief leaned over confidentially.

"Tell me what you suspect, ma'am."

"What I suspect...? I have no suspicions," she replied in surprise.

"Do you have full confidence in your servants?"

"Of course! I've known them for years. How dare you insinuate that there are bandits in my house!"

The chief apologized. He went on with his investigations at Don Antonio's house all morning long. The truth was that he could not make heads or tails of this theft with no theft. So as not to come off as bad at his job, he interrogated the inhabitants of the house again and again. From time to time, he shot angry glances at little Eva, who watched impassively as he came and went and grew ever more flustered.

"That brat knows everything," he said in a low voice to the scribe.

Later, disgruntled by his failure, he summoned the watchman, Rutilio. The latter humbly admitted that when he heard the first noises, instead of making his rounds of the corrals and the garden, he had retreated to the coal cellar and waited there for dawn. The man had seen nothing. The maids repeated the same story as before.

"Has everyone given their statement?" asked the police chief.

"Everyone except for poor Lorenza, who was so frightened she lost her voice," replied the lady.

"She lost her voice?" The chief pounced.

"Yes, sir," said the servants, the onlookers, and the lady of the house.

The chief, followed by the whole committee, headed

to the maid's room. Cautiously, he opened the door and went in. Lorenza, lying on her cane bed with her pink dress soaked in sweat, looked at them with eyes very wide from fear. When the Tiztla police chief put questions to her, she replied with staring eyes and moans, while fat beads of sweat dripped from her forehead. The chief seemed taken aback. When the church tower tolled twelve noon he ended the investigation, and he and the onlookers withdrew to eat lunch. They had seen and heard everything by then. The only plausible conclusion was that those strange visitors were Don Antonio's enemies. And what do enemies do, if not harm? For several days in Tiztla, no one talked of anything but these "enemies." As the wagging tongues polished them up, the enemies became ever more suspicious and strange, until one day they took the form of demons. Of course! That's why little Evita never wanted to say what she saw, and why Lorenza lost her voice.

The police chief typed up a report in which he detailed the demons' nighttime visit to Don Antonio Ibáñez's house. The report relayed all the extravagant shapes the demons had taken that memorable night, how they had destroyed a storeroom and a garden and made a "circle of infernal fire." The servant Lorenza Varela lost her voice because of what she witnessed that night, and the fact that authorities were never able to find out what it was only proves that it was something otherworldly.

The mystery was left locked inside Lorenza's muteness and Evita's silence. Today, many years later, I—Evita—have decided to tell the truth about the Tiztla theft.

The garden was the place where I liked to live. Perhaps because it was the toy my parents had given me, and it had everything: rivers, towns, jungles, ferocious animals, and infinite adventures. My parents were very busy with themselves, and they put us out in the garden and let us grow there like plants. And my siblings and I grew up, just like plants. For a time, my father was engrossed in remodeling the house: he made the walls higher and he built the storeroom. The house filled up with bricklayers, lime, and fresh concrete. My mother found those expenses useless. Then my father bought some sacks of corn, so he could put the useless storeroom he'd built to some use. I clearly remember the day the mule drivers came, and how my father joyfully directed the operation, which they carried out quickly. They leaned the six sacks of corn against the wall at the back of the storeroom. Then we all left, and my father very solemnly placed a padlock on the door latch, locked it, and put the key in his pocket. Everything stayed like that, untouched, for a long time.

In those days, between one September 16th and the next, a long time passed. I played in every tree, in every flower bed, on every hillock of land, until I came to the storeroom door. The sight of it unsettled me, and I tried many times to open it, in vain. My heart was heavy when I saw how fast it was aging, perhaps from sorrow that no one was ever going to open it. That abandoned door made me sad, and at some point I asked my father for the key to open it. But he had lost it, and the door remained locked, useless and melancholy.

I was very close with the maids at my house. I liked their black braids, their violet dresses, their shining jewelry, and the things they knew. Lorenza, the youngest of them, told me secrets on the condition that I told her my own equally important secrets. The only thing was, she was very hard to impress. Lorenza had an advantage over me: she was the daughter of a witch, and her knowledge of mystery was vast. I had nothing that could compare to all her mother's wisdom, except for my father's treasures. I explained that his Chinese vases cost more than a ship, though neither she nor I had ever seen a ship or knew what it really was. But we imagined it like a giant tower that spun around and gave off radiant light surrounded by water that was much clearer and bluer than the water in the house's fountain. When Lorenza learned that the vases were so valuable, she told me a secret of witchcraft, which I used to order my siblings around. When it started to get dark, I would go to the ironing room and talk to her. Steam rose off the clothes, and Lorenza's dark eyes shone in that heat. She told me terrible things, and then she'd drop the iron and sing songs of abandoned men along dusty roads sobbing in the night over ungrateful women. Her songs were very sad, and the room filled with tears and wayward birds. Then she added, "Julián is drinking because of me." And she started to laugh. I liked it when she laughed and I liked for her to talk; I liked to see her pale pink gums, her white teeth, and her opulent gold incisor.

"Mom, can I have a gold tooth?" I asked at night.

"Quiet! Don't talk nonsense, that's an awful custom."

One day I told Lorenza that I'd seen Julián with

Amparito. She threw the clothes to the ground and got angry with me. All the evil started with that anger. For several days I circled her, trying to please her.

"Go away! Don't come in here, you nosy little runt!" she yelled at me as soon as I peeked into the ironing room.

"But I still haven't told you where my father's greatest treasure is!" I yelled at her one afternoon through the crack in the door.

Lorenza was quiet. Then, from the rustle of the damp sheets, she answered:

"Well come in, then!"

I don't remember how much gold I told her was in the storeroom.

"Oh! So that's why your dad built it…"

"Yes, that's why."

"And if someone took all that gold, what would your father do?"

"Nothing, because he has a lot more."

"Where?"

"I'm not telling."

It was good to keep a trick up my sleeve, just in case she got mad at me again.

The night my mother had me stand on the chair, I saw Lorenza crossing the garden amid the torches of the intruders. She was wearing her pink dress and her braids were undone. She was running, terrified, looking for the way back to her room. Julián was behind her with a machete in his hand. I got down from the chair and didn't tell my mother anything. I thought it was better to wait for morning so I could talk to Lorenza. I went to see her very early.

"Damn it, Evita, it was empty! You're a liar. I swear on this"—and she kissed the cross—"I'm telling my mom, and you'll be dried up like a wineskin!"

I didn't know what to say. Her words terrified me. Lorenza sat up in bed.

"Plus, Julián almost killed me! And all because of a mouthy little brat! But my mom will cast a spell on you. And I'll see you in the market, hanging from a rope, just like any other dry wineskin!"

I didn't know what to say. I looked at her in desperation. Have any of you seen the wineskins drying in the sun in the Tiztla market?

"Julián and I will go to jail!" Lorenza moaned in a low voice, and she glared at me fiercely.

I looked down and felt my stomach slip away through a crack in the ground.

"But while I'm in there I'll be laughing my ass off at you, all covered in flies and yellow like a good leather hide."

"Oh, Lorenza, it's all so sad, me bewitched and you in jail…" and I started to cry.

"Don't cry, little Evita, I'm not going to curse you. I won't say anything to my mother if you don't say anything to yours," Lorenza replied, and she also started to cry.

"What if they ask us, Lorenza?"

"You say, I didn't see anything. And me, I've lost my voice from the fright…!"

Lorenza couldn't speak for many months, until her mother came down from the cuadrilla where she lived on the outskirts of Chilapa. She killed a rabbit in the place where the demons had appeared and taken her daughter's tongue, and she pronounced some words while she coated her braids in ash. From then on, Lorenza could speak with an animal tongue. And she still speaks with it to this day. I never saw Julián again. One day, amid all the steam from the clothes, I went up to her and asked, "What happened to Julián?"

"Huh! Imagine, child, he doesn't want to see me. He doesn't like women who speak with animal tongues..."

And it was true that her voice had changed. The rabbit tongue was too small, barely enough for her to speak in a whisper...

THE GNOME

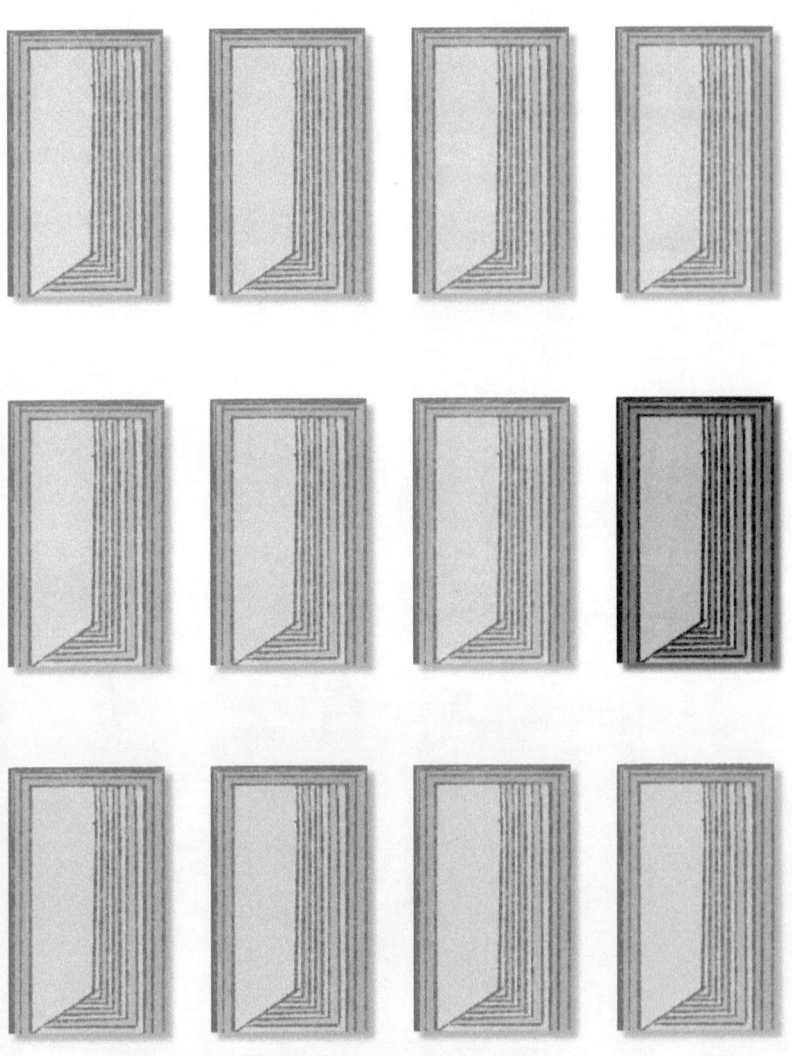

At three in the afternoon, the sun stopped at the midpoint of its cycle. The silence could shatter at any moment, and the garden could fall broken into a thousand pieces. The whole house was still, except for Rutilio hosing down the courtyard tiles. Seconds later, the water rose from the bricks as steam. The row of ferns that separated the garden from the covered gallery couldn't keep the burning wave of air from reaching the bedrooms.

Eva and Leli were rocking in two parallel hammocks. The hammocks' coming and going swung the afternoon with a sound of dry ropes. Every day at that hour, death circled them: it landed on the branches and peered down at them from there.

"Eva, are you scared of dying?"

"No, the other world is as nice as this one."

"How do you know?"

"Grandma Francisca told me."

Eva knew all. She was different; she was in the house

because she was curious about this world, but she belonged to a different order. She was a powerful ally, and the only link Leli had between this world and the sinister one that awaited her. "The other world is as nice as this one…" For a while those words convinced her, but then the door that awaited her and led to the void took shape again. With her very own foot, she would take the step that would send her flying into the abyss, to descend headfirst for all eternity in an endless plunge through the black pit that was death. Her father, her mother, and her siblings would also fall there. And they would never meet, because they would all fall at different times. Only Eva would stay floating in the garden, her yellow eyes watching the things that went on in the house.

"Are you sure the other world is as nice as this one?"

"Yes, and since we don't have a body, we don't sweat."

It was inescapable, this not having a body. Elisa said the same thing. The priest said it too. The body stayed here, and we couldn't even take a lock of hair with us to remember what color we had once been. She looked at Eva's golden hair. Near the temples it was very pale, and the sweat made it stick to her skin and take the form of very fine feathers. Eva was looking at her hands against the sun.

"We have light inside our hands."

Leli remembered the day she'd been playing with her father's razor and had cut a finger, and the blood had gushed out. She felt ashamed at catching Eva in a lie.

"Liar!"

"Haven't you seen Our Lord? A ray of light comes out

of each of his fingers. One day my fingers are going to light up and I'll go into the darkness."

It was true that Our Lord and the saints gave off light from their fingers and heads, and that Eva wasn't scared of the dark. Nor was she afraid of swinging from the highest branches of the trees.

"You'll fall!" Leli would shout when she saw Eva swinging from the high-up branches of the palm trees.

"If I fall, the Gnome will catch me," Eva would explain when she came down to earth.

The Gnome was the master of the garden, and he was a very close friend of Eva's. That's why, when their father scolded them for crushing the young bananas, Eva said, "Poor thing, he thinks he owns everything…"

That day, Rutilio went on watering the tiles, and three in the afternoon stayed written for a long time on the church clock that loomed in the garden's sky.

"Let's have a bath," said Eva.

They went into the garden, under the jacarandas, around the fountain, through the stand of banana trees as far as the palm trees, veering a little to the left to reach the well. The well was the coolest place in the garden; surrounded by ferns, cattails, and other plants, it oozed wetness. The sounds of the house didn't carry far enough to reach that secret part of the garden. A black stone parapet kept watch over its deep hole. Very far below ran the water of the rivers where silvery women and golden-feathered birds swam.

The girls got undressed and then raised buckets full of mysterious water. The icy water turned their bodies into two cold islands in the hot ocean of the afternoon. The water from the well was a laughing water, yet the girls bathed in silence. The afternoon was destined for what came next. Leli was looking at the leaves, which were always the same green leaves. Behind the elephant ear rose a plant of a darker green. Its leaf had red veins, and beneath the dark shade, a lighter green illuminated it with lustrous highlights. Leli plucked one of those beautiful, unfamiliar leaves and bit into it. The leaf was very sweet. She pulled off more and ate them. Eva always made the discoveries. This time it had been her. She was about to laugh in satisfaction, when she felt a needle piercing her tongue. She was still. Her gums started to grow and in that moment she remembered the black slave in *The Arabian Nights* with his scimitar at his waist as he gives out poisons to kill the favorite infidel women. "I am poisoned," she said to herself.

"Don't eat the plants, they're poisonous," Antonio would often tell them.

"Don't believe Dad. The Gnome is a good friend of mine and he's taken all the poison out of the plants," Eva whispered to Leli behind their father's back.

Eva had tricked her. "I'm poisoned," she said to herself again as she looked at her sister, who, unaware of Leli's fate, was still playing with the water. The presence of her approaching death astonished her. Soon she would start to fall headfirst for all eternity. Who would hold her hand? Not Eva, who was unaware of the inescapable evil that had befallen her, and would go right on delighting in the water. They had different times. They were in separate spaces, and with each second that passed their times grew further and further apart. The bonds that joined her to Eva loosened and fell soundlessly onto the grass. She would have to go into the other world alone. And all that separated her from her sister was a single green leaf. It is always minuscule things that set off catastrophes. She turned her final gaze toward Eva. But she couldn't say goodbye, or go alone, or leave Eva alone. An idea came into her head: kill her sister. She leaned over and broke off a stem of poisonous leaves.

"Evita, try these leaves, they're very sweet."

Her voice did not betray her treachery, and Eva accepted the gift gratefully. Would she know it was poisonous? She knew everything. "Dear God, make her eat them!" And God heard her, because her sister began to eat the leaves. What if they weren't deadly for her? Maybe the Gnome had taken the poison out of Eva's leaves. "Dear God, make her die!" And God heard her again, because suddenly her sister opened her mouth as though to say something, stuck out the tip of her tongue, and looked at Leli with very wide eyes, as her gaze changed from bewilderment to fear.

"You're wicked!"

Leli saw her run away. Her thin, naked body disappeared among the trees. A second cry reached her ears: "Wicked!"

Now Eva was in the same time as her. "The other world is as nice as this one, and we don't sweat there because we don't have bodies…" Was it Evita who had said those words to her? Leli fell down dead.

She was laid out in her bed and the white mosquito net was drawn. Eva was laid in the bed beside hers. Early in the morning, Leli opened her eyes and peered cautiously at the day of her death. In the other bed, Evita was looking at her in disgust; then she turned toward the wall. Leli watched as Elisa came into the room. She tiptoed over, opened the mosquito net, and felt Leli's forehead like when she had a fever. Then she drew back her hand, worried.

"Is what Evita says true?"

Leli realized that neither of them was dead, and she felt cheated. Eva lied. It wasn't true about her friendship with the Gnome, and she didn't really have powers. The green plant had hurt them both the same. Offended, she also turned to face the wall.

"It's not true, right...? You didn't really try to kill her," asked their mother, who as always didn't understand a thing.

Leli looked with visible distaste at the white lime of the wall.

"You didn't know they were poisonous. Right, dear?"

The girl sat up in bed and looked at her mother with serious eyes.

"Yes, I knew, and I asked God to help me kill her."

Elisa opened her mouth, stuck out the tip of her tongue as though to say something, and widened her eyes, as her gaze went from bewilderment to fear.

"Wicked!"

She hurried away from the bed.

"You're wicked!" Elisa repeated as she went over to Evita's bed. Her sister hugged their mother and they both started to cry. Their father came in and looked at Leli with frightened eyes. Then Estrellita and Antoñito came in. Her brother lifted up the mosquito net, winked at her, made his hand into the shape of a gun, and shot point-blank at her: Pow! Pow! Pow! Estrellita, alone and standing in the middle of the room, seemed astonished, as if she were very ashamed of her family and their crimes.

Their father hesitated at first, but after a few seconds he went to Eva's bed. The younger children followed him, and Leli was left alone, watched by her whole family as they listened to Eva sob in anguish. She and Eva were different again, but in a different way. Leli sat up in bed, also astonished. Why had the leaves hurt Evita the same? Her mother picked up her sister and carried her out of the room. Her father and siblings followed. Leli was left alone, thinking.

At noon she was served a thin broth. Candelaria looked at her with a bored expression.

"Come on, eat..." she said drearily.

Leli drank the broth, which tasted like a wet rag. She was bored, too. She tried to talk to Candelaria, but the woman only answered with banalities.

"When are you going to stop doing wicked things?"

Leli saw that Candelaria's nose was flat and that her voice was as boring as her expression. She was no longer interested in her advice: it was always the same. By sundown, her room didn't interest her at all. The herons had disappeared from the damp stains, and the corners were empty now. From time to time, she heard the sound of Evita's laughter and the Pow! Pow! Pow! of Antoñito's gun. Her parents' comings and goings intensified her boredom. They looked at her and asked the same question: "You didn't want to kill Evita, right?"

Her affirmative reply made them run away more frightened still.

When the lanterns were lit, Estrellita came in. She walked cautiously over, opened the mosquito net, and sat gingerly at the foot of the bed. From there she looked at Leli and blinked, as if her long lashes were so heavy that they tired out her eyelids. She didn't say a word. Estrellita never spoke, just looked. Leli observed her hands clasped on her little white skirt, her bare pink feet tangled in the veil of the mosquito net, her straight blonde locks falling over her shoulders. Motionless, imperturbable, she looked like a little golden idol. Leli had never paid attention to her. She sat up in bed to get a better look. Estrellita remained impassive as if Leli hadn't moved, or as if nothing Leli did mattered to her at all.

"Estrellita, tell me, have you ever seen the Gnome?"

"What gnome?"

"The one in the garden."

"No. I'm usually up on the roof."

"And you don't see the Gnome from up there?"

"No. From there I only see you and Eva."

"You always see us?"

"Always."

Estrellita looked like a Javanese doctor with her heavy eyelids, straight bangs, and bowed lips. Not a muscle of her face moved, and her hands, clasped solemnly on her little white skirt, were stock-still.

"Estrellita, I poisoned myself first. Then I gave the leaves to Eva and she was poisoned too. Why?"

Estrellita looked at her without blinking.

"Because they were from the same plant."

"Right! I know that. But why did Eva get poisoned?"

"Because you wanted to kill her," Estrellita replied, undaunted, looking at her sister. "Did you like killing her?" she asked, without changing her voice or her position.

"No...I didn't like it... Or maybe I did..."

Before that, she hadn't thought one could like or dislike killing. She looked at Estrellita with admiration.

"Then why did you kill her?"

"Because I wanted her to die with me."

"Oh!"

Rutilio came in with a pitcher of water with lemon. He set it on the nightstand, leaned over to look at Leli, and shook his head in disgust. Before leaving, he murmured a few words. Estrellita didn't move to look at him, or to pour a glass of cool water.

"Rutilio doesn't know anything," said Estrellita, who that day had not gone up to the roof to look at the garden and was there, in Leli's bed, hoping to learn what the others did not know.

"No, he doesn't know anything," Leli agreed.

Scarcely had Rutilio left when their mother came in, alarmed.

"Estrellita!"

She grabbed the girl's arm and pulled her out of the room. No one had understood a thing. Only Estrellita, because she watched from the roof. In the following days, Estrellita, on the rooftop, saw how the garden fell into ruin.

The banana trees, the jacarandas, the bougainvillea, and the ferns were covered in dust. Also from the roof, Estrellita watched the bored heads of Eva and Leli as they rocked in their hammocks without speaking. Estrellita knew that Leli now knew that Eva had no secret, and she wouldn't speak to her because she was a liar. Eva's tongue was still wounded, and she tried to ignore her sister. They both turned their backs on each other, while the garden fell into ruin.

One day, Estrellita realized that Eva had made a decision: from her hammock, she smiled mischievously at Leli. Estrellita saw the garden, for a few seconds, become for Leli what it had been before: radiant with aromas, exultant with foliage. But Leli remained unmoved in her hammock, and the dust fell over the branches again. Estrellita, incredulous, rubbed her eyes and waited. Those two could not be alone.

"Leli! Lelinca!" said Eva.

Her sister turned when she called, possessed by an emotion so violent that it reached as high as the rooftops.

"Lelinca, it wasn't you..."

Estrellita heard Eva's words from the rooftop and shook her head in disgust.

"No, it wasn't me..." Leli repeated in her dumb voice.

Her words reached the rooftop and Estrellita, with her hands clasped on her white skirt, knew Leli had forgotten that Eva didn't have a secret.

"It was the Gnome, he was mad at me," Eva declared shamelessly.

"It's true! It's true! He poisoned the leaves," cried Leli, opening her mouth like an utter fool.

Happy, she rose from her hammock. Estrellita heard how, for Leli, birdsong was soaring and golden coconuts were swaying among green palms. Disgusted, she shook her head. She, Estrellita, looked incredulously at the splendor of that love from her rooftop, and without unclasping her hands, she blinked several times in distaste. Her little white skirt shone like a mushroom on the red roof. Beside her, a roof tile was lifted, and the girl turned toward it unsurprised.

"You know it wasn't me, right?"

"Of course I know that! Eva is a liar and Leli is a killer. Just ignore them," said Estrellita in a steady voice, now accustomed to her family's crimes.

The Gnome took off his red cap, wiped the sweat from his forehead with the back of his hand, and from the open space of the raised tile, he looked with relief at his only friend: Estrellita Garro.

THE RING

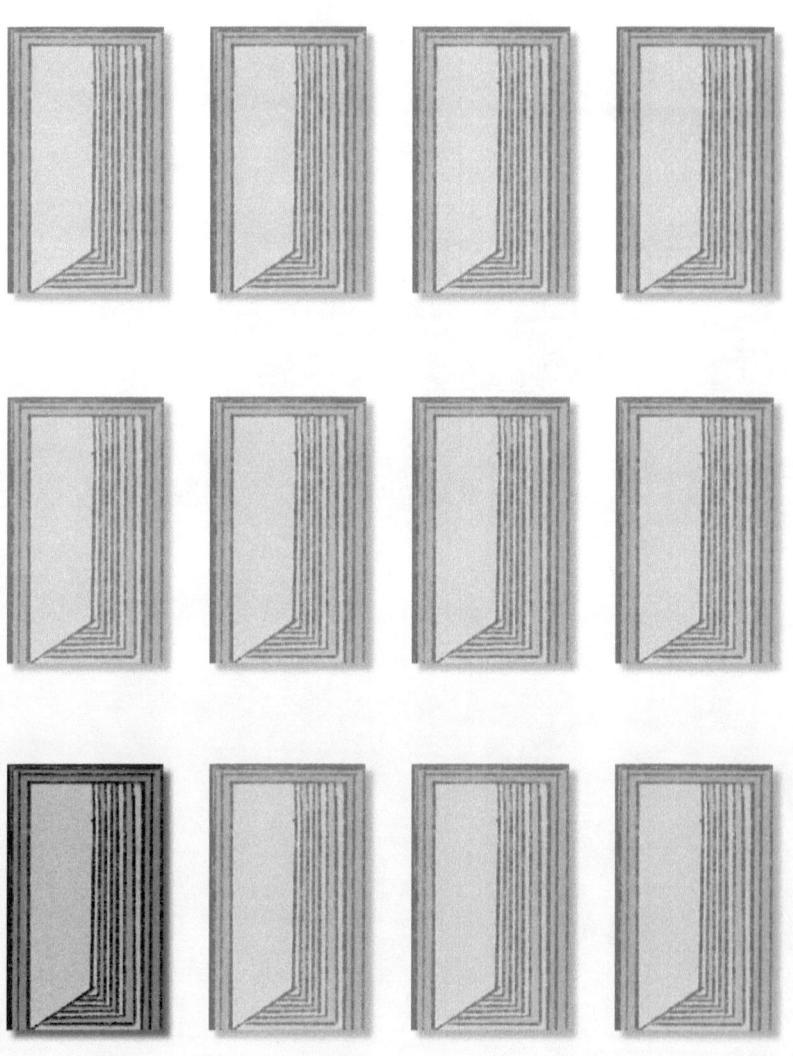

We were always poor, sir, and always unhappy, but not so unhappy as now, when woe runs rampant through my rooms and corrals. I know that evil can arise any time and take any shape, but I never thought it would come in the shape of a ring. I was crossing the Plaza de los Héroes, it was growing dark, and the ruckus of birds in the laurels was starting to die down. It had gotten late. What might my children be doing now, I wondered as I walked along. I had been traveling to Cuernavaca since dawn. I was in a hurry to get home because my husband, as happens when a woman marries badly, drinks, and when I am away he starts to beat my children. He doesn't mess with my sons anymore, they're big now, sir, and God forbid it but they could hit him right back. But he is brutal with the girls. I had just turned off the street that leads down from the market when the rain caught me. It rained so much that rivers swelled along the curb. I was trying to shield my face from the downpour when I saw my disgrace shining in the water running over the stones. It looked like a tiny golden snake lying there all stunned by the coolness of the water, with little eddies forming around it.

Look at that, Camila, a gold ring! I said to myself, and I leaned over and picked it up. I didn't steal it. The street is the street and what belongs to the street belongs to us all. It was very cold and had no stone: a wedding ring. It dried in the palm of my hand, and it sure didn't seem to be pining for any fingers, because it stayed still and soon grew warm. On the way to my house, I was thinking: I'll give it to Severina, my oldest little girl. We are so poor that we've never had any treasures, and my greatest luxury, sir, back before our lands were taken away and the damned pigeon-shooting ring was built right where we used to sow our fields, was the time I bought myself some black patent sandals with buckles to wear to my son's funeral. You must remember, sir, that day when Legorreta's thugs killed him over our land. We were already poor then, but ever since that day, without my lands and without my eldest son, we have truly fallen into misery. That's why any little treat is so special for us. When I got home, I found my children sitting around the comal.

"Hello, kids! How did you spend the day?"

"Waiting for you to come home," they replied. And I saw they had not tasted food all day long.

"Light the fire, we're going to eat dinner."

The children lit the fire and I got out the cilantro and cheese.

"How glad we would be with a bit of gold!" I said, building up to the surprise. "How lucky is the woman who can say yes or no while shaking her gold earrings!"

"Yes, how lucky…" my children said.

"How lucky is the young lady who can point her finger to show off a ring!" I said.

My children started to laugh, and I took out the ring and put it on my daughter Severina's finger. And there it all ended, sir, until Adrián came to town and started whirling his eyes around at the girls. Adrián does not work more than two or three shifts a week repairing stone fences. Other days he's in the doorway of El Capricho watching us buy salt and bottles of soda. One day, he stopped my daughter Aurelia.

"Hey there, girl, what's your sister Severina made of?"

"I don't know…" the innocent child replied.

"Hey, girl, and who is your sister Severina made for?"

"I don't know…" the innocent child replied.

"Hey, girl, and that hand that wears the ring, who did she give it to?"

"I don't know…" the innocent child replied.

"Look, little girl, you tell your sister Severina that when she buys salt she should let me pay, and let me look her in the eye."

"Okay, then," the innocent child replied. And she came home to tell her sister what Adrián had said.

The afternoon of May 7th was coming to an end. It was very hot, and work had made my daughter Severina and me thirsty.

"Go on, dear, and buy us some sodas."

My daughter went off and I sat on the patio of my house to wait for her to come back. As I waited, I noticed how the patio floor was broken and dusty. Being poor, sir, means you gradually crack like any brick that's been stepped on a lot. That's the way it is with us poor people, not a soul looks at us and everyone steps on us. You saw it yourself, sir, when my poor eldest son was murdered so they could take away our land. What happened? That murderer Legorreta built himself a palace on my land, and now he has his white silk kneelers in the village church, and every Sunday when he comes from Mexico City he fills it with his gunmen and their families, and we barefoot folk keep out to save ourselves the sight of so much disrespect. And from suffering so much injustice, the years pile up and our satisfaction and joy are swept away, and a person ends up like a pile of dirt long before the dirt ever welcomes us home. I was caught up in these thoughts, sitting on the patio of my house, that May 7th. Look at you, Camila, so down and out! Look at your children. How long will they last? No time at all! Before they know it, they'll be sitting right where you are, if they're not dead like my murdered little boy, their heads seething with poverty and the years hanging off them like stones, counting up the days when they didn't feel hunger... And I walked, sir, through my life, and I saw that all the paths were covered in my footprints. How much one walks! How many turns one takes. And all for nothing, or to one day find your son tossed into the cornfield with his head cracked open by rifle butts and blood pouring from his mouth. I didn't cry, sir. If a poor person started to cry, their tears would drown the world, because every day is a new reason to sob. Someday God will grant me room to cry, I was saying to myself, when I saw I was in the courtyard of my house waiting for my daughter Severina to return. The fire was out and the dogs were barking like they do at night, when the stones change places. I remembered that my sons had gone to Guerrero with their father on a pilgrimage to the Day of the Cross festival, and they wouldn't be back until the 9th. Then I remembered that Severina had gone to El Capricho. Where did my daughter go, that she hasn't come back yet? I wondered. I looked at the sky and saw the stars on their journey. I looked down and my eyes met Severina's, peering at me sadly from behind a pillar.

"Here's your soda," she said to me in a voice where affliction had just been sown.

She handed me the bottle, and that was when I saw her hand was swollen, and she wasn't wearing the ring.

"Where is your ring, dear?"

"Lie down, Mother."

She lay down in her bed with her eyes open. I lay beside her. The night passed and my daughter did not utter another word for many days. When Gabino came home with the boys, Severina was already starting to dry up.

"Who cursed her?" Gabino asked, and he withdrew into his shell and didn't drink alcohol for many days.

Time passed and Severina kept wasting away. Only her hand was still swollen. I am ignorant, sir, I never went to school, but I knew enough to go get Doctor Adame, who lives in Cuernavaca at Aldana 17.

"Doctor, my daughter is drying up…"

The doctor came with me to the village. I still have his prescriptions here.

(Camila took out some crumpled papers.)

"Mother! You know who made Severina's hand swell up?" Aurelia asked.

"No, dear, who?"

"Adrián, so he could take her ring."

Oh, that wretch! And deep down I knew that Doctor Adamo's prescriptions could not relieve Severina. Then, one morning, I went to see Leonor, aunt of that damned Adrián.

"Come in, Camila."

I went in carefully, looking all around in case he was there.

"Look, Leonor, I don't know who your nephew is, or what brought him to town, but I want him to return the ring he took from my daughter, because he is using it to curse her."

"What ring?"

"The ring I gave to Severina. Adrián took it from her with his own hands in El Capricho, and since then she is unrecognizable."

"How dare you come in my house and insult me, Camila. Adrián's mother is no witch."

"Leonor, tell him to give me back the ring, for his own good and the good of his whole family."

"I can't tell him what to do! Nor do I like my blood impugned."

I left and kept watch over my daughter all night long. You know, sir, that the only thing people give away is evil. That night Severina started speaking the language of the cursed. Oh, holy Jesus, don't let my daughter die possessed!

And I started to pray a Magnificat. My comadre Gabriela, who is here today, told me, "Let's get Fulgencia, so she can draw the evil from Severina's breast." We left my daughter with her father and siblings and went to get Fulgencia. Then Fulgencia spent all night long curing the girl, under the cover of a sheet.

"Before the first cock crows, I'll have gotten the evil out," she said.

And so it was, sir. Suddenly Severina sat up in bed and cried out, "Help me, Mama!" And she spat out an animal as big as my hand. The animal held little pieces of her heart in its paws, because it had been attached to my daughter's heart... Then the first cock crowed.

"See here," said Fulgencia, "now you have to get the ring back, because in three months the animal's young will have grown."

As soon as it was light out, I went to the fence in search of the wretch, and I waited for him there. I saw him coming; he wasn't whistling as he walked, and he kicked a stone in front of him. He had his eyes down and his hands in his pockets.

"Look here, Adrián, you stranger, we don't know where you came from or who your parents were, and yet we have received you warmly. You, on the other hand, go around hurting young women. I am Severina's mother, and I'm asking you to return the ring you're using to curse her."

"What ring?" he asked, cocking his head to one side. And I saw his eyes shining with enjoyment.

"The one you took from my daughter at El Capricho."

"Who told you that?" Now he cocked his hat to one side.

"Aurelia did."

"And has Severina herself said so?"

"How could she, when she is hurt?"

"Hmmm…! So many things are said in this town. Who would have thought, when it has such lovely mornings!"

"Then you won't give it to me?"

"Who says I have it?"

"I'm going to curse you and all your family," I swore.

I left him at the fence and went back to my house. I found Severina sitting out in the sun in the corral. The days passed and the girl started to get better. I was working in the fields, and Fulgencia came to tend to her.

"Have you gotten the ring?"

"No."

"The young are growing."

Six times I went to see the wretch Adrián, to plead with him to return the ring. And six times he leaned against the fence and delightedly refused.

"Mother, Adrián says that even if he wanted, he couldn't give the ring back, because he smashed it with a rock and threw it in a ditch. It was on a night when he was drunk and he can't remember which ditch it was."

"Tell him he must let me know where the ditch was, so I can go find it."

"He doesn't remember…" my daughter Aurelia repeated, and she looked at me with the very first sadness of her life. I left the house and went to find Adrián.

"Look here, stranger, you have to remember the ditch you threw the ring into."

"What ditch?"

"The one you threw the ring into."

"What ring?"

"You refuse to remember?"

"The only thing I want to remember is that in fourteen days I'm marrying my cousin Inés."

"Your aunt Leonor's daughter?"

"Yes, that's the one."

"This is recent news."

"So recent it's from this morning…"

"First you're going to give me my daughter Severina's ring. The three months are almost up."

Adrián stared, as if he were looking at me from very far away, then leaned against the fence and stuck out a foot.

"Now that's not going to be possible…"

And he stayed just like that, looking at the ground. When I got home, Severina had gotten into bed. Aurelia told me she couldn't walk. I sent for Fulgencia. When she arrived she told me that Inés and Adrián's wedding was set for a Sunday, and the families had already been invited. Then she looked sadly at Severina.

"There's no cure for your daughter. Three times we'll draw the evil out of her, and three times it will leave its young. You can do nothing for her."

My daughter started to speak the strange language, her eyes fixed on the ceiling. She stayed like that for several days and several nights. Fulgencia could not get the evil out of her, so it grew to its full size. And who could have told us, sir, that last night it would turn so evil? Fulgencia took out the second animal along with very large pieces of Severina's heart. She was left with just a little bit of heart, but big enough for the third animal to get hold of. This morning it was like my daughter was dead, and I heard the bells toll.

"What is that sound, Mother?"

"Bells, dear…"

"Adrián is getting married now," Aurelia told her.

And I, sir, remembered the wretch and the banquet he was having while my daughter lay dying.

"I'll be right back," I said.

And I went across town to Leonor's house.

"Come in, Camila."

There were a lot of people and many mole dishes and bottles. I went in and looked all around to find him. And there he was, with a cheerful mouth and serious eyes. Inés was also there, also cheerful, and there were all the Cadena aunts and uncles, all cheery.

"Adrián, Severina is no longer of this world. I don't know if she has a foot of earth left to sow. Tell me how to find the ditch where you threw the ring that is killing her."

Adrián started, and then I saw the ire in his eyes.

"I know nothing of any ditches. Plants wither from a lot of sun and not enough water. And girls from being made for someone and ending up with no one…"

We all heard the hiss of his angry words.

"Severina is drying up because she was made for someone who wasn't you. That's why you've put this curse on her.

156

Enchanter of women!"

"Doña Camila, it's not for you to know who your daughter Severina was made for."

He stepped back and looked at me with burning eyes. He didn't seem like that Sunday's bridegroom: there wasn't a trace of enjoyment left in him, no memory of laughter.

"The evil is done. It's too late to mend it."

That's what the stranger from Ometepec said, and he kept walking backward, looking at me with more and more rage. I moved toward him, as if to scratch out his eyes. He's going to disappear, I was saying to myself as I walked forward and he walked backward, as he got madder and madder. We went out into the street that way, because he was still leading me with the flames of his eyes. He's going to my house to kill Severina, I read in his mind, sir, because that's the direction he was headed, walking backward, feeling his way with his heels. I saw his white shirt waving, and then, when he turned the corner to my house, I saw it turn very red. I don't know how, sir, but I managed to hit his heart, before he could end my daughter Severina's life...

Camila fell silent. The man from the police station looked at her, bored. The young woman recording the statement in shorthand stilled her pen. Sitting in some wicker chairs, the relatives and widow of Adrián Cadena lowered their heads. Inés had blood on her chest, and her eyes were dry.

Gabino nodded in support of his wife's words.

"Sign here, ma'am, and say goodbye to your husband, because we're going to lock you up."

"I don't know how to write."

Adrián Cadena's relatives turned toward the door through which Severina had just come in. She was pale, and her braids were undone.

"Why did you kill him, Mother…? I begged him not to marry his cousin Inés. Now, on the day I die I'll be met by his anger for having separated him from her…" Severina put her hands over her face and Camila couldn't say a word.

The surprise left her mute for a long time.

"Mother, you left me all alone on my path…!"

Severina looked at those present. Her eyes fell on Inés, who brought a hand to her chest, to her pink linen dress, where she caressed Adrián Cadena's dried blood.

"He cried a lot the night Fulgencia took his child out of you. Then, in his sadness, he wanted to marry me. He was an orphan and I was his cousin. He was mysterious in his loves and his ways…" said Inés, lowering her eyes as her hand caressed Adrián Cadena's blood.

After a while she was given her young husband's pink shirt: sewn into the fabric over the heart was a ring like a little gold snake, and engraved on it were the words ADRIÁN AND SEVERINA IN GLORY.

PERFECTO LUNA

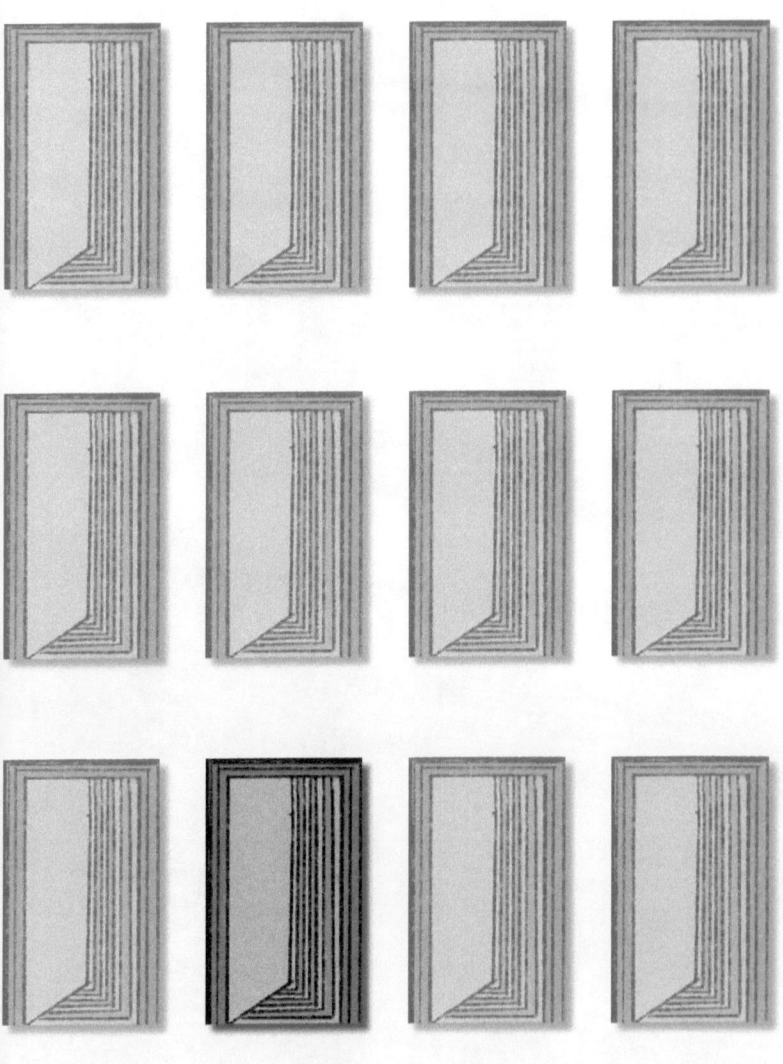

It was perhaps eleven-thirty at night when Perfecto Luna passed the town's last houses. At that hour everyone was asleep and no one saw him go by. It had all been very simple, thank God: lift the bar across the shop door, poke his nose out through the crack, and then emerge onto the dark street. Hopefully the place won't be robbed, he thought, then people will say, Just look what a scoundrel Perfecto was, he went and stole everything there was in the store. But what else could he have done? He didn't want to give up his life to an erratic soul! Especially after seeing that the other world held nothing but a cold wind. Now he had no choice but to flee, to erase all trace of himself in the town and on the roads, throw away his name and find another. Leave no sign of Perfecto Luna. But what name should he take? It wasn't so easy to stop being himself. He'd had his name since he was little. He had always been Perfecto Luna, the builder, the laborer, the kid who was handy at everything, because that's what his boss had taught him to be. Now he had to forget what he knew and start over again as someone else. He felt sorry for himself: he had been so helpful and so happy! But that's life: to each his own good or bad luck. He recalled his friends' names. Crisóforo Flores: there was no way he could take that name, it would mean stealing his friend's very soul. And yet, perhaps he would have to. Crisóforo was always so confident, so cheerful, so free of sorrow—just like Perfecto had been before. Domingo Ibáñez was risky, for that man's nights were sad. Not Justo Montiel, either, lest he start killing his friends.

He left the sidewalk to head into the fields and go off-road toward Actipan. That way, when everyone was looking for him in San Pedro, he would already be in Acatepec, carefree. He liked the Acatepec market. As soon as he got there, he would buy a good silk handkerchief and start looking for work. After all, he was handy at everything. It would take him all night to cross the acacia-dotted fields, but it was safer that way. Who could track him through the brush? He quickened his step and stumbled over a rock. "Oh no, Perfecto Luna, now you've gone and stubbed a toe!" he said aloud to himself, wanting to frighten off the round silence that surrounded him just then. It was better not to look; the fields had become huge. It was starting to happen again, the thing that had happened every night for the past five months: the silence was growing so intense that it was useless to try to say a word; never, throughout the ages, had a noise rung out in that place. He had just said, "Oh no, Perfecto Luna, now you've gone and stubbed a toe!" and yet he hadn't said it. The words had come out silent and were left dangling from the tip of his tongue. He had to get far away from Amate Redondo and far from Perfecto Luna, because it was Perfecto Luna who was wanted; that's why he'd been stuck there in those round nights that lasted longer than the day. He sped up again. The layers of air parted; his nose was in the empty space between two of them, and he could hardly breathe. On the other hand, at the height of his eyes and his hair, the wind blew without blowing, making his hair stand up and turn cold, until he felt like thousands and thousands of icicles were piercing his head. When would he finally get away from these strange places? I will be Crisóforo Flores, I'll get out of these parts, and I'll once again enjoy life with my friends, he told himself.

Ahead of him he saw a man who was bent over, looking for something in the acacia. He was leaning very low over the ground, trying to see in the darkness. Perfecto Luna was pleased to find another person in those lonely parts. The man was there, two steps away, blocking his path. Out of politeness, Perfecto said hello.

"Hello," the stranger replied, without pausing in his search.

"Are you looking for something?" Perfecto Luna asked graciously, thinking that that was how Crisóforo Flores would say it.

"Yes," said the stranger in a plaintive voice. "And I can't find it…"

"May I help you, sir?" Perfecto Luna asked, feeling ever more Crisóforo Flores.

"If you'd be so kind…" replied the other man in a faint voice.

Perfecto Luna bent over to look for the lost object.

Surely it was money, and the crafty man didn't say so out of fear that Perfecto Luna would steal it. He could barely see amid the shadows and the rocks. He looked curiously at the stranger's legs; he seemed to be wearing huarache sandals and a red tilma. He also seemed to have trouble moving, as though he were blind. He groped around laboriously, clutching onto rocks and brush.

"Oh, sir!" said Perfecto Luna, again feeling like the words barely left his mouth. The man ignored him and went on searching, moving rocks aside.

Perfecto Luna sat down on the ground, discouraged.

"Oh, sir, such things have befallen me!" he went on, forgetting to be Crisóforo Flores. "Look what I've become, I'm down to skin and bones!"

The confession did not move the stranger, or make him rise from his position.

"You know, I was Perfecto Luna until tonight!"

"Goodness, I'm tired of searching and searching!" the stranger complained.

"I'll help you," Perfecto offered, remembering that he was supposed to be cheerful Crisóforo, and he threw himself energetically into the search once more. The stranger was far off now, and Perfecto could just see his white-and-red shape searching amid the acacia. He felt at ease in the man's company. He thought, This will be my last wretched night; starting tomorrow, once I'm Crisóforo Flores, no one will ever remember the person I was.

"Sir!" he called optimistically, feeling like it was tomorrow already. "Do you believe in the dead?"

"In the dead?" the other man asked in surprise. His voice reached Perfecto from far below.

"Yes, sir. Not the dead with earthly bodies, but the others…"

"The others?" the stranger asked, pausing in his search.

"Yes, the others," Perfecto replied with aplomb, ever more Crisóforo Flores. "Just think, I was Perfecto Luna, and I had to stop being him all because of a dead man!"

"Oh!" replied the stranger.

"Did you pass through Amate Redondo? You must have met Don Celso, the owner of the grocery there. Everything I was I owe to him. He taught me to work when I was Perfecto Luna. I was running errands for him by the time I was five years old. I grew up with him, because I was born an orphan: Come, Perfecto, this is how you plane the wood! Stand here, Perfecto! You know how much a measure of corn costs, now mark it on the register! Because only Don Celso has a register in Amate Redondo. He is the only person who has worked enough to have one, even if people say he skims grams from a kilo. And that's how I went through life, working, up until Don Celso wanted to build those damned extra buildings."

Perfecto Luna fell silent. He remembered how confident he had been up until that day. Don Celso told him to demolish the shacks that were behind the grocery and to build some houses like the ones in Mexico City. And he went back there with the hoe in his hand, knocking down those huts. How long did it take him to do that job? Let's say a month; at the end of that month, everything was razed and clear. Up to that day, too, he had been cheerful. What was his life missing? Nothing. He was treated well and had the respect of his friends. No one wished him ill. It was April 4th when Don Celso told him, "Dig some trenches to pour the foundations." At around noon that day, as Perfecto was deepening that ditch, he found the dead man. He was an old dead man, because only his bones were left. Perfecto could just see him now, shining in the sun with his arms folded over his ribs. He must surely have had a bad death, because he has no head, Perfecto had thought. Who could have killed him? Where was his head?

"You see, sir, his head was missing, he must have been beheaded!"

The stranger didn't say a word.

"The bad thing is, sir, that when I was Perfecto Luna I liked to be mischievous. Perfecto!, Don Celso's wife shouted, come and eat! I put my blanket over the hole with the dead man and went to lunch. I remember how while they were passing the tortillas, I was holding back my laughter.

"What's so funny? they all asked me.

"That's for me to know, I replied.

"And only I knew. After lunch I wrapped the bones in my blanket and brought them to my room. Just wait, you dead bastard! I said. The day came when I put up the adobe walls..." and Perfecto could just see himself there, stirring the mud with dried plants, whistling.

"Look at that one, what a joy to see, if only they would all work like that! Don Celso said. And it was true, because when I was Perfecto Luna, I liked everything, and everything made me happy. I remember I was rolling my cigarette when the idea came into my head. I went to my room, took out the big toe bone, and stuck it into an adobe brick that I had set out to dry in the sun. Since someone's already done you the favor of burying you in pieces, I'm going to finish what they started, I told him. I made a mark in the adobe, so I would know that one piece of the grave was there. Then I took out a rib and put it into another brick marked with a symbol. And so on until I was out of bones.

"Hey, Don Celso, what happens to a dead man who's broken into pieces? I asked.

"Well, he goes crazy, kid, looking for all his pieces.

"Ha, ha, ha! and I went around merrily to my little graves. Oh, what it is to be young and cheerful, sir!" said Perfecto Luna, sitting back down on the ground and looking around for the other man, who was still indifferent, ignoring him. Sadly, he thought how no one cared that he, Perfecto Luna, had once been cheerful, and that because of his cheer he'd had to stop being himself. He remembered how he'd started to build the houses: carefully, he distributed the adobe bricks with bones into the walls of all the houses; there wasn't a single place in the neighborhood where the "headless one" was not buried. And he went on blissfully fashioning windows, putting on roofs, making doors, while he whistled and laughed to himself.

"Oh, Perfecto, they're looking beautiful! Go ahead and add the blue wainscoting."

"I painted it the most brilliant blue, sir, to brighten up the drywalled grave."

And he laughed again in spite of himself. Hopefully the Juárezes will come live here, and at night the "headless one" will tug at their feet, he thought. When the houses were finished, Don Celso told him to watch over them, to keep any kids from sneaking in and vandalizing the walls. It all smelled new, of lime and concrete. The walls and brick floors were still damp; all the rooms held the clean presence of things untouched by man. Perfecto Luna took his shirts, his sleeping mat and blanket, and he settled into one of the rooms. He was tired; he took off his huaraches, lay on his mat, and looked out the window at the night. The sky was calm and clear, and from where he lay he saw two bright stars. He half-closed his eyes. Who would have thought I could do this whole job alone! He opened his eyes and looked joyfully at his work: he scanned the ceiling, the walls and the door, then turned back to the window. Below it, a small protrusion marked one of the "headless one's" graves. He started to laugh, and then his laughter curdled. His lips stiffened, and the room grew so dark he lost sight of the window. Who darkened the night? He fumbled around for the candle he had left beside the sleeping mat. He reached out his arm and discovered it had gotten very short; the room, on the other hand, had grown enormously, and the candle was far out of reach. He resigned himself to darkness. He opened his eyes wide, trying to see something, but the shadows grew ever denser. I think this place is haunted, he said to himself. He went still. Suddenly, he saw the shine of the mark he had left in the adobe. It's the headless one! His heart started to pound so hard it was like he was in a very swollen river. He felt like he was going deaf. All he could do was wait for dawn to come. But the night dragged on for many nights. When day finally broke, he saw that his sleeping mat was soaked in sweat.

"What's wrong with you, Perfecto? You look all out of sorts."

He didn't know what to say. He could barely sip his coffee, thinking how the day would inevitably grow dark again. He sat sadly on the patio by the extra houses to watch the sun glinting off their roofs.

"The day is already coming to an end…" he said sorrowfully. He moved his mat and belongings to the second room. The night returned and he lay down, unwilling to look out the window.

This time I'm not going to look at the night, he thought, and he squeezed his eyes shut. The sound of wings swept across the walls. The wings circled, rising and falling around the room. They brushed over his forehead and over his body. He grew freezing cold. Which of those damned bones made that noise that couldn't be heard? That night lasted even longer than the one before. He wanted to think through how to placate the dead man, but the wings moved so fast that they kept him from forming thoughts. At dawn, his knees were aching and he could hardly stand.

"You caught cold, Perfecto," they said.

And he could not tell them what had happened during that immense night with those cold wings. He turned toward the sun, but his knees stayed stiff and cold. He had no time to warm up, because that day the sun did not last long. It seemed that no sooner had the cock crowed at sunup than he heard the chickens settling into their roosts to sleep. Utterly desperate, he moved his sleeping mat, his blanket, and his candle into the third room.

You damn dead man, keep still and don't disturb my peace! I've never done any harm to anyone!

He rolled up in his tilma to ward off the cold and closed his eyes so as not to see the shadows that surrounded him. A whirlwind came out from a corner of the room; it whirred violently and came to hit against Perfecto's left ear. And in it rushed, disorienting him.

Tell me, vile dead man, what do you want me to do for you? is what he would have liked to say, but the words got stuck on his tongue. Then his tongue was bandaged, the way they'd bandaged Anselmo's leg when he got cut with a blade. Motionless, his tongue bound, he suffered through that whirlwind that made his body cramp up.

"Morning has come..." he struggled to say when he went into the kitchen for hot coffee.

"What's wrong with you, kid? Why are you talking like that? It's like your tongue is tied up."

And Perfecto Luna lowered his head and thought how that day, as well, was going to end very soon.

"Don Celso, will you let me sleep with Alambritos?"

"You must be joking, kid, what do you want him for? You got the jitters?"

He'd hardly had time to grab Alambritos when night had already fallen. He used a long rope to tie the dog to the door handle of the next room he was to sleep in, and he lay on his mat. He was growing skinny, and his laughter had died! The darkness started to descend from the ceiling like a thick black cloud that wanted to crush him. What do you want me to do for you, dead man? I can't tear down the buildings to gather your bones together again. He had just finished this thought when he saw Alambritos crawling toward him with his belly flat on the floor like a pancake, to then cower beside Perfecto. From his new shape squashed and flat like a sheet of paper, Alambritos started to howl. Then it's true that you're here, thought Perfecto Luna. What do you want? I'll give it to you so you'll go away. At that moment, the layer of shadows fell over him like a heavy blanket and left him with no more thoughts. The dead man wanted *him*! All night long he lay there under that black blanket.

"Look, kid, your nose is all flattened!" he was told when he came out of the room. His legs could scarcely hold him up.

"Don Celso, how long does a night last?"

"Same as every other night."

By now the days were but a flash of light between two immense nights. He didn't even have time to put on or take off his huaraches. His clothes began to grow old on his body. No chance of ever trimming his mustache or hair! As soon as he got up in the morning, night was there already! He didn't have time to eat, and he was whittled down to skin and bone. He went down the line of rooms until he ran out, and in each of them he found the dead man who wanted to scare him out of his skin. From where he sat besieged on the patio, he could hear Crisóforo in the distance, playing the harmonica and singing with friends. They must be at the cantina. That knowledge only plunged Perfecto deeper into sadness, because it announced that night was there, lying in wait for him.

"What's wrong with you, kid? If you keep on like this, it won't be long until you give up the ghost."

"Don Celso, will you let me sleep in the grocery?"

That way, the "headless one" would wander furiously through all the new outbuildings without finding him, since he would be sleeping amid the bundles of cinnamon and bags of corn.

"Go ahead, but if you're doing this out of fear, you won't escape it there."

Perfecto Luna moved his sleeping mat into the grocery. It seemed like that night arrived more peacefully. The shop was lively: the customers were drinking their last glasses of tequila; Don Celso was figuring up accounts; it smelled of alcohol and spices. Perfecto felt relieved. Ten o'clock struck, and his friend Crisóforo Flores tossed back his last drink.

"I'll see you tomorrow—if you wake up, that is, because your face is starting to look like a dead man's…" and Crisóforo headed off nonchalantly, his hat cocked to one side.

Don Celso said good night. Perfecto Luna closed the doors to the general store, noticing how greasy they were, and drew the bar that went from one wall to the other across the door. Then he lay down on the counter, leaving the kerosene lamp burning—with the light on, the "headless one" wouldn't dare. Delightedly, he breathed in the smell of lard mixed with bean dust, and he felt safe as he stretched out. Then he heard a noise coming from the back storeroom. He looked for the candle and matches, but he'd left them in the pocket of his coarse cloth shirt. The noise grew louder. It was wiser not to go see what it was. A similar noise joined in with the first: something was falling, falling nonstop, whistling sweetly. It was as if two sacks of corn were letting the grains out through a hole.

Oh no, the wretch has gone and opened the gunny sacks!

The whistling grew. All the sacks were emptying out fast. The storeroom was filling up with corn, he was sure of that. Cautiously, he looked over: the door to the storeroom had been overwhelmed by grains, and the corn was surging through it into the store. Astonished, he looked around. He was surrounded by jute sacks, and the wooden shelves above the door were piled high with them. Just then the first sack opened and the grains began to spill onto the floor in a muffled golden stream. Then a second sack split, then a third, then a fourth, then corn was raining down from all the walls of the store. The space around the counter was shrinking. He saw that the front door he had barred so carefully would soon be blocked, as holes were opening in the sacks above it. He got up as best he could, and with long strides, sinking into the grain up to his thighs, he reached the door. Laboriously, he lifted the bar and managed to open it a crack, poke his nose into the night, and slip out onto the street.

"By this time, sir, I would have been buried in corn, and the cursed 'headless one' would have me by the short hairs for all eternity. But I got away from him. And I got away not just from Amate Redondo but from Perfecto Luna, because when the 'headless one' looks for him he won't find him anymore. I'm Crisóforo Flores now. Oh, what it is to have a little presence of mind. Isn't that right, sir? That's why I asked if you believed in the dead, because before the 'headless one' I didn't believe either."

"Oh!" replied the stranger from very far below. And now he straightened up with difficulty.

"I'm going to help you look, now that I've told you the sad story of the man who was Perfecto Luna."

"No need!" replied the stranger, now standing beside him. Perfecto scarcely had time to see his new friend's faceless face: the stranger's body ended above his shoulders.

"He was bedeviled!" Don Celso said the next day. "He emptied all the corn sacks and died out in the acacia. My oh my, and he seemed like such a good kid, that Perfecto Luna!"

THE TREE

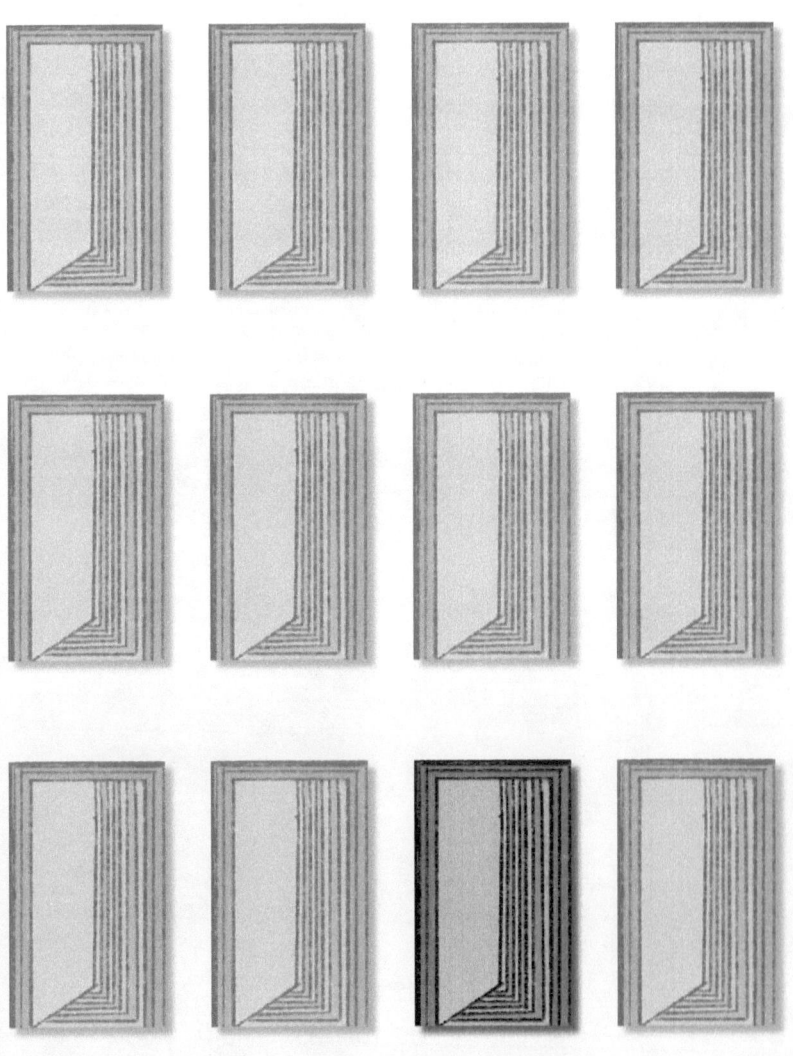

Saturday at three in the afternoon, Gabina left. It was her day off, and she wouldn't be back until Sunday morning. Marta watched her go, and once she was alone, she locked herself in her room. She looked at the perfume bottles and the untouched china on the dressing table. Her house, with its thick carpets and drapes, isolated her from noise and streetlights; its silence weighed on her, and it felt to her like abandonment. Some of the beds were never slept in, some windows no longer opened, and the only ceremonies she ever attended were those of farewell: funerals and weddings. The ringing of the doorbell pulled Marta from her thoughts. Cautiously, she crossed the house and went to the door.

"Who is it?" she asked, unsure whether to open it.

"It's me, Martita," said a childish voice from the other side of the wood.

"Luisa…?"

Marta opened the door to let the Indian in. The woman's shadowy black bulk slipped quickly into the salon; she

entered in a flash, dodging the furniture and glancing side-
ways at Marta. Her angular face was scarcely visible in the
gloom created by the drawn silk curtains. She dropped into
an armchair and waited. A sickening smell emanated from
her. Marta looked at her blackened, bare feet, worn from so
much walking.

"What's going on, Luisa? What brings you to Mexico
City?"

Luisa leapt back to her feet, lifted her underskirts, and
showed Marta a huge bruise on her fleshy groin; then, agi-
tated, she sat back down and pointed to her black-and-blue
nose and the trickle of black, half-dried blood coming from
her ear.

"Julián!"

"Julián?"

"Yes! Julián beat me!"

"That's not true, Julián is a good man!" And Marta
remembered what Gabina said: "A good man gets a bitch for
a wife." Luisa was a bitch, a dog who followed her husband
around until she drove him crazy. The Indian woman met
Marta's eyes and crossed her arms over her chest.

"He has always beaten me, Martita…! Always!"

Her voice squeaked like a rat's. Marta was sure that
Luisa was slandering her husband. She had known the couple for many years. She saw them whenever she went to her
country house in the village of Ometepec. When she first
met them, she'd thought that Luisa was a child-woman; it
wasn't until much later that she noticed Luisa's laughter and
behavior were not just strange, but evil. She lost all fondness

for Luisa, and never missed a chance to treat her harshly. It incensed her to see how that woman followed her husband around with such stupid tenacity. She didn't leave him alone in sun or shadow; wherever he went, there she was, smiling and malign. Everyone loved Julián, but no one sought out Luisa's company. He had resigned himself to tolerating her. The Indian woman began to laugh and looked at Marta maliciously, as if she could tell what she was thinking.

"Quit laughing!" Marta barked at her.

"Julián is evil, Martita, very evil!"

"Shut up, no more of that nonsense!"

She would have liked to tell Luisa that she was hateful, and that if Julián really had hit her then she must have deserved it, but she held back.

"He *is* evil, he makes me cry!"

"Look, Luisa, you are someone who laughs and cries easily. And you know what I say? That if Julián hit you, you deserved it."

"No, I don't deserve it. He is evil, truly evil…"

She insisted on accusing him. Her meanness was nauseating. Her stench spread through the salon, permeated the furniture, slid down the silk curtains. "Just smelling her is punishment enough," Gabina had said, and it was true. Marta looked at her with disgust. Luisa leapt to her feet again, and, as was her habit, started to cover Marta in kisses. Then she stopped and went back to the sofa. Marta saw some squalid tears rolling down her cheeks, but she felt no compassion at all. The Indian wiped the tears away with a dirty finger, crossed her arms like a little monkey, peered at her distrustfully, and added:

"He always hits me, always. He's evil, very evil, Martita."

The two women were silent and looked at each other with hostility. Marta turned toward a mirror to inspect her well-groomed hair. She was disturbed by the repugnance the Indian woman inspired in her. My Lord, how can you allow human beings to take on such attitudes and forms? The mirror reflected back the image of a lady dressed in black and adorned with pink pearls. She felt shame in the presence of that unhappy woman, so bewildered by misfortune and ravaged by the misery of ages. Is it possible this is a human being? Many of her friends and relatives held that Indians were closer to animals than to men, and they were right. She grew more nauseous. Why did she have to listen to this woman? It was too late, she was there in her salon, and Marta just throw her out. She heard Luisa crying behind her. She would give her something to eat, since she could not offer affection. She couldn't let her keep sitting on the sofa, under the weight of all her misery, all her helplessness and ugliness.

"Luisa, do you want something to eat?"

"Don't you put yourself out, have Gabina get me something."

"She's not here, it's her day off."

"Then don't put yourself out, Martita."

Ignoring her, Marta headed for the kitchen. Luisa followed, sat down beside the window, and waited. In the afternoon light she looked even more horrible: her face was like a trampled fruit, with the dried blood mixing with the fresh blood trickling from her ear to form clumps in her black hair. Her smell invaded the corners of the room, the aluminum pots and pans, the sink, the blue chairs. Marta poured her some hot coffee, served her chicken and bread. Then she moved closer to the door to escape the smell, which was starting to make her dizzy. She looked at Luisa with rage, and the Indian woman shrank down in her chair and started to cry.

"I left my children…!"

"Bitch! How dare you talk to me about your children? Poor things! Always crying: Mommy, leave Daddy alone, stay home with us… And you, what do you do as soon as they're born? You're back out there, chasing after Julián. Don't tell me you're crying for them now."

"Yes, Martita, I'm crying for them."

"Well, your tears don't move me. Why do you chase Julián? The poor man complains you don't leave him alone even to do his business."

Marta was silent and looked at the Indian angrily. The other woman smiled gently.

"Out there it's not like here, Martita. Out there we go to the ravine."

"What does the ravine have to do with what I'm saying?"

Marta stamped her foot on the floor; the Indian's slyness made her furious, and she felt herself turning red from rage.

"The ravine is very dark, Martita, very dark…"

Luisa's voice sounded strange in the radiant kitchen. Marta kept quiet and peered at her closely. The woman started to cry and pushed her plate away.

"You don't know what darkness is, Martita. There's a lot of light here, but out there it's dark, very dark…and the dark is ugly, Martita."

She was like a cornered animal. Marta now felt compassion for the creature, for the only thing she was capable of understanding was fear.

"Yes, I know, Luisa. Be happy, there's plenty of light here. If you want, you can stay here with me for a few days. Where else are you going to go? No one cares for you."

"It's true, Martita, no one cares for me."

Who could love this woman? Marta felt her revulsion return. The smell was invading her house, it clung to her nose and turned the air sticky. She went to her room to breathe in the perfume enclosed within its walls. How should she tell Luisa to bathe? If she didn't, the whole house would be contaminated by that smell of old bile, blood, and sweat. She looked in her closet and found some well-worn clothes. They would serve as a pretext to get Luisa to bathe—the old woman would happily accept the command if it came with a gift. She went back to the kitchen and found Luisa staring at her plate.

"Luisa, when you've finished eating, take a bath. You look very tired."

Luisa leapt to her feet and widened her eyes. She went over to Marta and took her hand.

"Where, where, Martita?"

"Where what?"

"Where do I bathe, Martita?"

"Wait, there's no rush, when you've finished eating…

And here, you can put on these nice clean clothes…"

"Thank you, Martita, thank you. May God repay you. I have my own clothes. I brought them with me when I left my house and found myself alone in the middle of the world… I didn't have anywhere to go. I went walking along, walking, and suddenly, in the middle of the fields, Martita appeared to me, and I thought: I'll go to her, she's so good…! And that's how I came here, with Martita's face always before me, guiding my steps…"

As she spoke, she untied one end of her shawl and took out some old, clean clothes. She shook them in front of Marta:

"Look, all the color is gone from them."

Marta hid her own garments behind her back, and didn't know what to say.

"I'd better bathe now, Martita, so I won't disgust you so much."

Upon saying these words, she stared at Marta: she seemed ashamed, and she also seemed to want to shame Marta.

"Disgust me…? Luisa, for God's sake, don't say that!"

"If I do say it, Martita, it's only because it's true. Where should I bathe?"

Marta turned red. The Indian had seen her revulsion.

"Where, where?" she insisted malignantly.

Marta ceded to Luisa's imperative voice, and, under its sway, she led her to the door of the yellow bathroom.

"I'll show you how to use the shower…"

"I know, Martita, I already know how!" Luisa replied, pushing her out of the room.

"How could you know? Your village doesn't have bath-rooms…" Luisa closed the door without answering.

"Stupid old woman, you'll burn yourself!" Marta shouted furiously and pounded on the door, but the Indian had locked it. Resigned, Marta went back to her room. She'd have to wait until Luisa came out of the bathroom of her own accord: she'd break everything in it and burn herself in the process. She was a savage unacquainted with modern advancements. Luisa took so long to bathe that Marta fell asleep in an armchair. From her sleep, she heard someone talking on the phone.

"Martita is sleeping in a chair…"

Startled, she got up and went to the next room, where she found Luisa talking into the phone. When she saw Marta, the Indian hung up the receiver and smiled at her. Her damp hair was down and she wore a clean dress. The smell had dissipated.

"You're infuriating! Why did you answer the phone when you don't know how to use it?"

"I do know, Martita, I do know how!"

Marta didn't want to contradict her. But how could she know, when Ometepec didn't even have electricity? Luisa was crazy. She must have heard the phone ring and picked it up out of curiosity: when she heard a distant voice, she'd started to chat with it like a madwoman, and now there she was, looking very contentedly at Marta, her hair loose and her eyes full of mischief.

"I'm going to finish eating dinner, Martita."

Night had fallen, and Luisa had turned on all the lights

in the apartment. Marta checked the time: it was eight o'clock. She headed to the kitchen to make something to eat for herself, and there she found Luisa crying over her plate.

"He's evil, Martita, evil!" she insisted again.

"Shut up! You're the one who is cursed!" Marta shot back.

"Cursed, Martita?"

"Yes, cursed. Why do you chase Julián?"

"I don't chase him. I take care of him because he's a coward."

"A coward? Now you're slandering him. Julián should follow his children's advice: leave. He should leave you and go far away."

"Leave me? Go far away?"

Luisa's beady little eyes flashed at her from the corner. She seemed startled, and no longer inclined to slander anyone.

"Yes, leave you, because you are bedeviled."

"Bedeviled? But I've only seen him twice!"

"Seen who?"

"The Evil One, Martita!"

Luisa had seen the devil two times. Perhaps if Marta got her scared about the Evil One, death, and the beyond, then she would start to behave better.

"Oh, so you've seen him twice! Well, be careful…the day you die, the devil is going to chase after you the way you chase after Julián."

Luisa looked at her furiously, then shrank back into her chair and pushed aside her plate. Marta watched out of the corner of her eye. Seeing Luisa's foul mood, she placed her own dinner on a tray and prepared to withdraw. She wanted to leave Luisa alone to reflect. The fear would make her change her behavior.

"What one owes in this life is paid in the next. You think about what I'm saying to you, and when you go back home, you behave."

She felt an urge to laugh and hurried to the door. Luisa didn't answer and threw her a dark look. Before she left, to dispel the bad impression, Marta added, "Be good!"

And in spite of herself, she burst out laughing. She always did laugh with the Indians. They were like her, they liked to laugh, and when she went to Ometepec, she was met by a chorus of laughter that she joined in with.

"Go on now, Martita," Luisa replied somberly.

Marta went on laughing in her room. Poor old woman, what a fright she'd given her! It was easy to deal with the Indians: all you had to do was mention the devil, and then you could do whatever you wanted with them. She finished her dinner but didn't feel like going back to the kitchen. It struck her that there was something strange about Luisa: the woman's smell had dissipated, and in its place a heavy air had left the curtains and furniture immobile. She really didn't know why she had felt like laughing. She couldn't pinpoint Luisa's strangeness exactly. She remembered her cowering in the kitchen, looking back at her with those beady, tenacious eyes. For years, Marta had considered her the village idiot; when she scolded her, Luisa would laugh and then kiss her with such zeal she seemed like a madwoman.

Often she'd felt that her scolding filled Luisa with rage and that her kisses, which seemed so childish, were heavy with hatred. "Crazy people are evil. They think everyone is after them and that's why they chase after everyone else. Luisa is crazy, ma'am," Gabina would say as she handed Marta the bath salts and the rosemary-scented towels. And it was true, there was something peculiar about Luisa, especially that night. It was as if all her years of suffering had taken on a tangible form, manifesting into a new, dark being. Marta was frightened by her own thoughts, and she looked around to be sure that it was only fear that was making her think such extravagant things. The clear order of her room restored her calm. Luisa slanders her husband because she is very unhappy; I won't get scared over nonsense.

Marta's thoughts were interrupted by the sound, scarcely audible, of bare feet walking over the hallway carpet. She froze. Luisa appeared in the doorway, small and shrunken, showing her very white teeth in an ambiguous smile.

"Martita!"

"Yes, Luisa…"

"The first time I saw the Evil One, it was before…"

"Before what, Luisa?"

"Well, before I killed the woman."

There was a long, astonished silence. Luisa had killed a woman? Where, when? And she said it just like that, so calm and in such a childlike voice? Marta felt she had to say something in reply, to stop Luisa from looking at her with those intense eyes, while the same fixed smile hung on her lips.

"You killed a woman?"

"Yes, Martita, I killed the woman."

"Oh, Luisa, such things you say!"

She wanted to pretend that it seemed natural for Luisa to have killed a woman. The Indian kept staring at her and laughing silently, with just the smirk of laughter, as if she were listening to something Marta couldn't hear.

"Martita, I'm listening to your thoughts..." she said in the same childish singsong. And she trotted over to Marta and sat soundlessly on the carpet at her feet.

"Fear is very noisy, Martita," she added. And then she was quiet. The two women knew that they were face-to-face in a house alone, cut off from the world by silk-papered walls and carpets that muffled any sound.

"The first time I saw the Evil One was before I married my first husband."

Luisa once had had another husband! Marta was learning that she knew nothing about the woman seated at her feet.

"When I saw him, I was in the corral at my house. He was a cowboy who breathed fire; he didn't have boots, he had horse hooves, and when he walked they drew fire. He carried a whip in one hand and he used it to lash the rocks, and the rocks spat fire. It was four in the afternoon and I started to scream: He's there! He's there!

"Who is supposedly there? my parents asked, because they didn't see him. The Evil One heard me scream and came closer, and his eyes spat fire.

"He's there! He's right there! I kept screaming.

"Who's there? my parents asked again, because they still

didn't see him. And the Evil One started to whip me before I could say his name... After that, I was always shaking and afraid. During that time my first husband came and asked for my hand, and my parents gave me to him, happily, to see if that would bring some relief... And we came to Mexico City..."

She had lived in Mexico City, and Marta hadn't known. Luisa stared at her. She seemed very aware of Marta's surprise, and it delighted her. Sitting on the floor, huddled over like a little animal, she narrowed her eyes to hide the sparks of malice.

"I lived right here in Mexico City, in Tacubaya...and I had my baby here. But I got all swollen up, Martita, and three days after I gave birth, my husband took me back to the village and left me at my parents' house. She wasn't swollen when you took her away, why are you returning her that way? they asked.

"Go to hell! he told them, and he left and I never saw him again. But my parents didn't know that. After a little while I said, See here, Father, I'm going to find my husband. And my father burst into tears. Leave the baby with us! he begged me.

"Of course! Did you think I would take him from you? And that's how I came back to Mexico City and lived in Tacubaya again, and here I was..."

Luisa paused her story to peer at the other woman. Marta didn't know how to meet her gaze, so she lowered her eyes and waited. Luisa lifted her skinny arm. "I lived right here!"

And she pointed into the air, as if Tacubaya were there

in the room with them. Marta was silent with dread. She sensed that the Indian woman's confidences were motivated by some interest she still couldn't discern. She had to stop her from continuing her tale.

"Luisa, don't tell me anything more, it's best to forget…"

"No, Martita, it's best to remember. This is where I lived, and this is where I met the woman!"

She paused again, and Marta felt she didn't have the strength for words. Luisa's voice and the silence of the house weighed on her. What did Luisa want from her? Why was she looking at her like that? She was a whore!

"And this is where I killed her!"

When she said these words, her voice and face became childlike. She had killed, and she said so with such an innocent air. Marta regretted having treated the Indians so leniently: seated at her feet was proof of her mistake. The old Creole loathing of the natives rose up violently within her. They deserved only the whip! She looked at the Indian and felt safely ensconced in her principles.

"And why did you kill her?"

"Because she was going around saying things…"

"What things?" Marta asked in a hard voice.

"Just things… That I had been with her husband, who I didn't even know…" When Luisa said this, her little eyes lit up: like most women, she had no sense of guilt. She was innocent before Julián, before the dead woman, and before the dead woman's husband. Marta looked at her with rage.

"I didn't even know him…! I had never even seen him, and she said things…" Luisa said, scratching her head to convince herself of the truth of her words. Then she raised an index finger. "Look here, woman, don't go around talking that way, or else you'll find silence in my knife! That's what I told her, but she didn't listen. Do you think, Martita, that she didn't understand? Then I went to find her at the market, at the time of day when we all go to buy things. And it was nice! Full of onions, cilantro, limes. I stood right next to the women selling tortillas, and since they were kneeling, I saw her coming. That ungrateful woman came along swinging her basket full of fruit, and I thought to myself, I'll make you shut up, chickadee… and I buried my knife in her."

Luisa stopped talking. Marta was sure that her silences were premeditated. Frightened, she breathed in the heavy air accumulating above their heads in the wake of Luisa's words.

"Oh! Luisa, how could you bring yourself to do such a horrible thing? How could you bury a knife…?"

"Well, I put it in her belly, Martita. Where else is as sure and as soft as the gut?"

With a sudden movement, Luisa took out a huge knife she'd hidden under her blouse and mimed the movement of stabbing it into an imaginary belly. Marta barely had time to stifle the scream of horror that threatened to rise from her chest and burst out. Speechless, she watched Luisa disembowel a nonexistent being. She had dropped her childish ways, and her eyes had a phantom shine.

"Like that, like that," Luisa repeated, panting, as she went on jabbing at the air. "And there she stayed, and I ran away…"

"You ran away..."

And Marta saw her running among the people at the market, her hair flaming behind her, the same cruel eyes she had now, and the knife in her hand. The people made way, only to run after her. Killing must be a terrible moment; maybe it has its grandeur, Marta thought to herself.

"And I left the market and ran down the street... I still had the knife in my hand when I entered the house where they caught me, and it was all covered in blood!"

"You didn't leave it in her?"

"No, Martita, I took it out because it was mine. And it was covered in blood...! Do you think, Martita, that it spattered me...?"

With her fingertips she caressed the knife blade, then raised her eyes and fixed them on Marta's. She scratched her head as if to shoo away a thought and went back to caressing the knife, lost in her memories.

"A person has a whole lot of blood...we are fountains, Martita, beautiful fountains... That's what she was like, like a fountain in the morning at the market... You see it, Martita, a morning, with its market and its beautiful fountain?" Luisa's voice took refuge again in its childish tone, and she smiled affably.

"And who was she?"

Who was this woman, Marta wanted to know, who had ended up lying on the ground one morning in a distant market, her basket overturned and her fruit rolling in blood, the cries of vendors and the smell of cilantro all around her?

"Oh! Well, who knows about that..."

"What was her name?"

"Who knows!"

Luisa realized Marta was interested, and she didn't want to give any of her dead woman away. She kept her jealously for herself, and hid her name and face. Marta was irritated.

"What do you mean, who knows?"

"Right, Martita, who knows. She was just the woman who said things: that's why I stabbed her with this knife…"

Luisa placed the knife at her feet and fixed impassioned eyes upon it. Marta saw that it was useless to ask about the woman, and she looked at the shining weapon that Luisa had buried in a stranger's taut belly.

"With that knife?"

"Yes, Martita, with this one. They took it away when they caught me, but later I cried so, so much, that they gave it back to me along with my freedom."

Marta thought the Indian must be lying. It wasn't plausible that they would return the murder weapon to the murderer. Luisa must want to scare her because she had defended Julián. She was wily as well as jealous. Marta felt ridiculous for believing the woman's stories. She imagined how the two of them would look to an observer: a couple of old women scrutinizing and scaring each other in a shadowy room with a knife on the floor. She started to laugh. Luisa was a liar, and Marta looked at her mockingly.

"And did you go to jail?"

"Sure, Martita! They locked me up; they took away my freedom. And that was where I saw the Evil One again…"

Back to the "Evil One": there was logic to her story; she

must be telling the truth. Marta realized she had provoked these confessions herself by telling Luisa she was bedeviled. She'd wanted to scare her, and all she had done was open the door and let Luisa's demons out. Her worry returned.

"Yes, Martita, I saw him again there. He was painted on a wall, like this, as tall as me! And he was double, a man and a woman. It was my job to flog him, and they handed me the whip. Every day I pummelled him until my hand shook. And when I finished lashing him and couldn't even move, another inmate would say to me, Go on, Luisa, hit him another little while for me! And I started whipping him again, because you can't deny a favor to a fellow inmate. After they released me, I never saw him again."

"Never? That's good, Luisa! You must be happy to be free of the devil and of prison."

"No, Martita, life in lockup wasn't bad: we rose at four in the morning and started to sing; then we ground the nixtamal for us and for the male prisoners; then we bathed. That's why I told you I knew how showers worked. See, Martita, see how I wasn't lying to you? The showers in prison were just like yours, except they weren't yellow."

She was speaking in a low voice now, and she said the words "inmate" and "lockup" with a passionate tenderness.

Her eyes had filled with nostalgia. She grew sad, and the knife glinted uselessly at her feet. She looked at Marta sweetly.

"Work was never finished: we'd clean the pots and pans where they used to cook the prisoners' food…we washed clothes, stairs, hallways…"

"And how long were you there, Luisa?"

"Who knows! I came to forget the outside world. I was only with the other women, my companions. I found my home there, and I had no sorrows. I grew so complacent there that the nights and days flowed like water. If we got sick, there were two doctors—two, Martita! And they took care of us. I stayed so long that I no longer recognized any other house…"

She looked sadly at Marta and was silent. Now her pauses were involuntary. It was strange to see her so melancholy as she evoked her time in prison.

"I used to answer the phone. You see how I wasn't lying to you, Martita?"

"It's true, Luisa, you weren't lying."

Suddenly Luisa grew animated again, laughing.

"At night there were dances in the corral. The male prisoners took out their mandolins and guitars and we danced, we danced. I had never danced before, Martita! A poor person's life is not dancing, it's trudging over stones and it's hunger. My companions taught me the steps; they put my braids up on my head and said, This way you'll look less Indian. And we danced and danced…"

Her look turned dark again, and Marta felt uneasy.

"When they told me they were going to let me go free, I didn't want to. What for, sir? I asked. Where would you have me go? And I stayed right where I was. But they told me again that I had to go. One woman told me, Go on, Luisa, take your freedom! And although I didn't take it, they forced it on me. What do I do now, Doctor? I don't know the outside world anymore, and I don't have a penny to my name, I said. The outside world is made of coins, Martita, it's all coins out here. The doctor gave me money for my ticket, and the woman who'd told me to take my freedom came to wait for me at the door to the world, and when I found myself in the street, she took me to the train and I went to my parents' house…"

Her face darkened when she said this. She started to cry disconsolately. She looked very old, her face etched with wrinkles and her skin dried by sun and dust. Marta was silent.

"But I didn't recognize it, Martita! Oh, Luisa, this house is no longer yours, I said to myself. And I just sat there thinking about the women who had been my companions and about what they would be doing right then…"

Her voice dissolved into sobs.

"But how long were you in there, Luisa?"

"Locked up…? Who knows! But it was a long time. Didn't I tell you, Martita, that I no longer recognized the street or the world? When I got to my parents' house, my baby had grown this big."

Luisa raised her arm and marked in the air the height of a ten-year-old. She stayed suspended there, lost in memories: she saw her years of imprisonment as her most favorable time. She talked about it the way others evoke lost palaces, riches, or youth. Now that she was returning home in her memories, her face had turned hostile. She stopped crying.

"And what did your parents say?"

"Nothing: How are you, daughter?"

"No, what did they say about your time in prison?"

Luisa jumped to her feet, went on the alert, and stared at her.

"About my time as an inmate? Nothing! They never knew. No one ever found out! They believed I had been living in Tacubaya with my first husband."

"But didn't your husband go back to the village?"

"No! I was lucky, he was killed by one of the prisoners who got out of the men's jail. And he never, ever went back to the village to say a word. There are things, Martita, that no one must know. No one knows I was in prison: not my parents, who are dead, and not Julián. When he asked for my hand, I didn't tell him a thing; I pretended to be a widow, and a widow is what I am."

She hunched over again and peered at Marta. The two of them were silent. Why was Luisa telling her this story? They looked each other in the eye, spying on one another's thoughts. The noise of the little gold clock on the dressing table was quick: time made its presence known, charging at them with exceptional speed. Luisa straightened up a little.

"Before I got out of prison, my fellow inmates, who cared about me so much, told me, Look here, Luisa, never tell anyone that you killed that woman. People are bad, very bad. That's what they said. We know you're going to feel tempted to tell people. A person feels obliged to confess their sins, their own sins. You have your own and they are yours alone; and you also have the woman's sins, and together they will weigh heavy on you. You know, Martita, that a person carries the sins of the people they have killed.

197

That's why you see men who shoulder two or three deaths and are bent double under the weight. But don't tell anyone, Luisa, and don't say a word about where you've been all these years, either! That's what they told me and that's what I did, Martita; you're the only person I've told. But look here, Luisa, my companions told me, if you ever feel like the sins are buckling your legs and emptying your stomach, go to the country, far away from any people; find a leafy tree, embrace it, and tell it whatever you want. But only do this when you truly can't stand it anymore, Luisa, because you can only do it once. And that's how it went, Martita; time passed, and only I knew what my life had been. Until my legs began to bow and I couldn't handle food, because my sins and those of the dead woman, which outnumbered my own, sat heavy in my stomach. And one day I told Julián, I'm off to chop wood! And I went into the hills and found a leafy tree and I did just as my companions had instructed. I embraced it and said, Look, tree, I'm coming to you to confess my sins, so you can do me the favor of carrying them. And there I was, Martita, and it took me four hours to tell it what I had been…"

Luisa was out of breath, and she paused her story to look furtively at Marta, who was very pale. What was this Indian getting at? She felt her heart pounding, but didn't dare raise a hand to her chest. Motionless, she waited for the end of the story.

"I returned to my house, and it was a long time before I went to see the tree again. And when I finally did…" Luisa fell silent and looked at Marta. "I saw that it was dead, Martita."

Silence fell between the two women, and the room filled up with beings who sliced the air with tiny knives of dry wood.

"It died?" Marta murmured.

"Yes, Martita, it dried up. I had burdened it with my sins…"

The dead tree entered the room; the entire night dried up within those desiccated walls and curtains. Marta looked at the clock: it was also withering on the dressing table. She searched her memory for a banal gesture that she could direct at Luisa, who, petrified by her own words, was looking at her, crazed.

"Easy now, Luisa, when I said you were bedeviled, I was joking! The past doesn't exist anymore. We never go back to being what we were."

The Indian woman didn't move. She was looking at Marta from many years back, and Marta was afraid.

"Don't be scared, Luisa, we're both happy here and what happened is gone. You can't go back…"

"It dried up, Martita, it dried up…" Luisa repeated.

"You already told me, Luisa, stop repeating yourself. Go on and get some sleep! The two of us are safe here, far from everything…"

"We're so alone here, Martita…!"

"Why do you say that, Luisa?" Marta asked in a voice hollowed out by fear, aware of the immobile silence of her furniture and curtains.

"Because Gabina isn't coming back till tomorrow…"

"Luisa, go to bed… You know where your room is…"

Marta wanted to be alone, to break the spell. Luisa smiled and picked up her knife. Marta cried out, "Leave it!"

"Why, Martita? It's mine."

And in one gentle motion she made it disappear under her blouse. Slowly, she abandoned the mistress's room and left it in stillness. Marta waited a few minutes: nothing stirred in the house. She got up and moved the jars around on the dressing table, and the hairbrush fell to the floor. The noise did not assuage her fear, however: from the shadows, people were spying on her movements and laughing at her, and she was swinging in the void. She started to get undressed. From a black tunnel, people were laughing at her with peals of inaudible laughter. She got into bed: she wanted to trick her enemies, make them think she wasn't afraid. And she turned off the light. Why had she told the woman that she was bedeviled? She had only returned Luisa to her past. How strange that she had been so happy in prison! There, she'd been the equal of the others. What was the Indian doing now? She would have liked to go and spy on her. She was sure Luisa wasn't sleeping, either. She was scared, too. She spied on Julián out of fear, fear that he would leave; the countryside doesn't have doors, and she couldn't lock him up. She was frightened by her own freedom and that of others. Stupid old woman! All those Indians were the same. She had no love for them, and only tolerated the ones who flattered her, like Gabina. Sometimes she was kind to them out of laziness, but the depths of her heart held an irreparable hardness. In jail, Luisa had found peers and learned to dance; out in the world, she'd

returned to her place and could only put her trust in a tree...
"and it dried up, Martita, it died..." She heard Luisa's voice
repeat the same words inside an infinite tunnel. She was in a
cold sweat and turned on the light. She looked at her initials
embroidered along the edge of her sheet. She regretted not
having a gun: she would shoot Luisa like a rat! If she looks
in at my door, I'll say to her, See here, Luisa, I'm praying,
and she'll come and pray with me. Murder was an act of solitude... She listened again, but didn't hear a sound; maybe
the Indian was sleeping now. Where would she have left her
knife? She didn't seem to ever put it down. It was the key
that had opened the door to equality, to dancing and joy.
It was her talisman. The silence convinced Marta that the
other woman was asleep, while she was still deep in thought.
She looked at the clock, which showed two in the morning.
She longed for the dawn. From now on she would be stricter
with the Indians. Suddenly, the little hands ran frenetically
and made a deafening racket. Inside that noise, Marta heard
bare feet on the carpet.

"Luisa...! Luisa...! Luisa...!"

There was no response, and the phone was in the other
room. The footsteps had stopped in the middle of the hallway. She wouldn't have time to get to the door to lock it.
Luisa would leap at her like a wildcat.

"Luisa...! Luisa...! Damned Indian!"

She heard the bare feet again, and covered her face with
her hands.

Gabina arrived back at her mistress's house at six in the
morning. It wasn't until eight that she noticed something

strange had happened. She found Señora Marta in her bedroom: she had been dead for over five hours. The police found Luisa hiding in a neighboring house, the bloody knife in her hand. They took her to the Tacubaya prison.

"None of my companions are left!" said Luisa, after checking all the cells and patios. And she sat down to cry bitterly. She had forgotten that, between her release and her return, over a quarter of a century had gone by. Martita was right: We can never recover the past.

MERCURY

For Ernesto Flores

I'm sure now of the first time I saw the woman. It's odd, it was like I saw her and didn't see her. I was troubled that day; a man doesn't make life decisions lightly. In the moment, we can't tell if it's us making the decision, or if someone else decided for us. "She is sooo wholesome!" my mother had said to me before I left the house. Her words irked me. It was growing dark, and the streetlamps on Paseo de la Reforma got muddled up with the evening light. The giant headline of a newspaper: HIS RENUNCIATION MUST NOT BE ACCEPTED made me almost trip over the newsboy. These politicians interfere even when I'm on my way to speak with Don Ignacio, I thought to myself resentfully as I dodged the kid, who looked at me with terrified eyes. No sooner was I over that obstacle than I again heard my mother's perfidious words: "She may not be pretty, but she is sooo wholesome." My mother accentuates her sentences on the word "so"; it's unmistakable. It was her ambiguous and emphatic "so's" that caused my rage and distraction, not Carlos Madrazo's renunciation.

We all get married one day, and Ema adores me, I told myself as I passed the statue of Charles IV. I remembered how at the Jockey Club, at the movies, at her house, she always looked at me and took my hand. If any of her girl-friends smiled at me, Ema would squeeze my hand, and later in the car she would reproach me: "I have my dignity, you don't do that to *me*!" She is a girl with a lot of class! Maybe this was the quality that bound me to her. Why would my mother say she wasn't pretty?, I wondered as I reached Avenida Madero on my way to her father's office. I had never thought of her as sooo wholesome! Well, you don't marry the prettiest girl, but the one who loves you most. "It's a way to move securely through life," Don Ignacio had told me. And yet it bothered me that my mother found her ugly.

I went into the building, and when I got on the eleva-tor I wanted to think about Ema, but to my shock, I could remember absolutely nothing about her: her voice, her body, her face, they had all been totally erased from my memory. I only felt, against my cashmere suit, the compact weight of her body when she kissed me. Shocked, I raised my eyes and looked at the lighted panel that displays the floor number. A red two appeared, then gave way to an equally red three. It was just then that the woman's perfume reached me, metal-lic and intense. I looked down and to my left. How odd! I'd thought it was just me and the elevator operator. Now it turned out that this woman was there too. I looked at her domed forehead, her nearly platinum hair, her straight nose, and her eyes fixed on the display panel. Then I looked at the panel too: we were already at the eighth floor. I looked back at her. Where had I seen her silvery dress before, her long neck and thoughtful mouth?

"At the New York Metropolitan Museum of Art," she told me, without turning her head or moving her lips.

Really, she didn't say it out loud…though I'm not so sure of that. I think perhaps I remembered it myself. She'd been standing on the stone steps, peering up at the white sky and the falling, powder-white snow that enhanced her hair with a twinkling halo and coated the walls and the black trunks of the trees in Central Park. She is a metallic woman, I'd thought to myself that day, observing her frozen nose and crossed arms. Her fur coat was flecked with metallic scales made of snow, and her whole being shone like a chiseled jewel in platinum, presiding over the snowfall…

Suddenly, in the elevator, I realized it was absurd for me to remember her, because I had never been to the Metropolitan Museum of Art, nor even to New York. She must be a gringa, and I must have seen her around here…I thought, smiling to myself. I looked at her again. She kept her eyes fixed on the panel, very serious. Her skin shone like a camellia, or rather like a white glove fitted over a perfect hand and arm. I heard her laugh.

"No, I'm not a gringa…" she said, or I thought I heard.

Now I saw that her dress was not made of silver, but rather of light gabardine. It was the cut that made it look silvery. I examined her from head to toe. She was as tall as me, and her shoulder brushed against mine. She wore her hair short, and her ankles were very slender. I looked at her mouth; she wasn't wearing makeup. How pretty! I thought, and I felt wretched. A light blue vein ran up her neck like a delicate path and disappeared between her ear and her light hair. I've seen that path before, I thought, feeling cold delight waft over the back of my neck. I remembered the balcony: it was narrow, made of stone, and she was there. I approached from behind to kiss the blue vein on her neck, which melded with a sky that barely entered through the narrow opening of the tower. Before my lips could reach her skin, she threw herself over the ledge. The pines below were embroidered with snow, and I, a young widower, stood there heartbroken, weeping tearlessly over my tragedy, which now in the elevator became unbearable. To avoid looking at her, I turned back to the numbers on the panel, which now showed 1715. I wasn't alarmed—everything breaks in Mexico. The elevator flew like an arrow, crossing the sky like a rocket. The numbers on the panel jumped around out of order and then settled on the number 14. The elevator stopped. I stopped as well. I turned to my companion, who was still gazing impassively at the panel.

"Floor fourteen, sir…!" the elevator operator told me in an impatient tone. His voice expelled me from the elevator. I found myself in the hallway with a waxed rubber floor. I immediately called the other elevator, wanting to go down and wait, to find out who that stranger was. The other elevator's doors opened.

"My apologies, Javier…! Were you leaving already…? I couldn't get here any sooner…" said a jovial voice that dragged me down the hall: it was Don Ignacio.

We went into his office with its red leather furniture. In one corner a ficus's boring leaves invaded the wall that was lined with grayish plastic. Two fat men in armchairs shook the same newspaper that had almost made me run into the newsboy.

"They're making such a fuss!" said Don Ignacio.

Immediately, the three men got caught up in an animated, obscenity-riddled conversation about cows and accounts.

"We'll have to congratulate Pancho discreetly…!" said one of them, rubbing two fingers together to symbolize money.

"His campaign was magnificent! I don't understand how they're sneaking in headlines like *this*," said one of them, pointing to the enormous letters: HIS RENUNCIATION MUST NOT BE ACCEPTED.

The man speaking was my uncle Ricardo, and the other was his partner, Don Joaquín. Both had been in politics, and their fortunes were incalculable. "Ricardo certainly did get lucky, to be blessed with such talent for stealing!" my mother would say whenever she talked about her brother-in-law. I don't understand why, but at that moment I didn't recognize either of them. Perhaps because, ever since my future father-in-law had led me down the rubber hallway, a great sadness had fallen over my shoulders. I had just lost something precious, something irretrievable… The conversation among those three friends, which yesterday would have made me jump for joy, now left me indifferent. I looked out the window, where the sky's blue heights were hidden by gloom, and I heard a phrase of music that made the leaves of invisible trees whirl…

"Madrazo wanted to take us back to the Stone Age…!" the grandiloquent words in the office hit the windowpanes like drops of wheatpaste. They were words I had heard since childhood: "Stone Age," "pack of Indians," "he set me up," "a little grease fixed it"… Now the three men were repeating that obtuse language over and over.

"Don't worry, Don Ignacio, I'll cover that…" I suddenly heard myself saying.

Don Ignacio seemed satisfied. The conversation had moved on from Madrazo, and now the subject was wedding expenses. It was all meticulously deliberated: floral decorations, music, drinks, reception. The guest list was drawn up, and last names were shuffled in with brands of wine.

"At least a glass of champagne," my uncle Ricardo opined. His proposition was met with silence. "At least a glass of champagne," he repeated several times.

"I'll cover that," I heard myself saying again.

The three men went on with their calculations. I looked at the newspaper and its headline: HIS RENUNCIATION MUST NOT BE ACCEPTED. What if I renounced the wedding— would it provoke the same outcry? I sank deeper into the armchair: I lacked the strength. At that moment, my elders were blending me into a past of theirs, which felt obscene to me; the brothels filed past one after another, and the names of women who smelled of talcum powder and cooking spices followed me back out to the rubber hallway. Once on the sidewalk, I hurriedly said my goodbyes.

"Ema is going to San Antonio tomorrow to buy her trousseau... Don't make that face, her mama's going with her..." added Don Ignacio, looking at me mischievously.

I had forgotten Ema, and I didn't care in the slightest whether she went with her mama or not. I refused Don Ignacio's invitation and watched him walk away with his friends: they were going to celebrate my wedding and Madrazo's renunciation. The last word I heard from them was the name of a well-known prostitute.

I walked down Calle Madero and went into Sanborns. I would eat something and then go to a movie. I didn't feel like being reachable by telephone: I wanted to avoid Ema. Ema is a heavy name! I thought while I ate some enchiladas. And starting that instant, my sole intention was to renounce the wedding. But how? I had gone too far to turn back now. I paid the bill. As I was crossing the perfume department, I saw the young woman from the elevator again: she was holding a beautiful bottle of bath salts, bracing and translucent like her.

I was distracted during the movie. The world was not as obvious as it seemed; another, unsuspected world existed opposite the one I lived in, and it was there that love, music, and beauty all took place... It seemed like that other world was unreachable for me because I lacked the key to enter.

I was going to get married, and I had never thought that love could be anything other than what Ema offered me. What did she offer? A stubborn presence and a fortune...

When I left the cinema, a freezing wind blew along Avenida Juárez. There were still vendors out selling

Madrazo's renunciation in large letters. I felt that the head-line had aged tremendously in just a few hours. It was my own renunciation that should be on those gray pages…

I slept poorly that night: I traveled to unknown places where the sad dead wandered. I woke up ready to break it off with Ema, but the days started to pass and I didn't take any steps toward achieving my ends. My mother was satisfied, everyone was satisfied, and I let myself be carried along by events that rushed ahead at dangerous speeds. Ema came back from San Antonio, and I didn't much like her sug-gestive looks as she showed me her "equipment." How to tell her about my decision to renounce the wedding? While I searched for the right moment, the external world went on at the same pace as always, except that things would suddenly take unexpected turns: one morning, the sky in the plaza opened up into a beautiful tunnel through which strange and luminous beings paraded; a few seconds later, they went up in columns of quicksilver. Another time, when I was coming out of the City Government Office, my path crossed that of the young woman from the elevator. I had gotten used to running into her. I saw her everywhere: on Paseo de la Reforma, or on a solitary street in Las Lomas; on the tennis courts, playing with astonishing precision, while I missed the ball because I was following her meticulous game. Who was she? Her silvery silhouette had become familiar to me, and if I hadn't been so overwhelmed by my impending wedding, I would have spoken to her—though she didn't seem open to any approach, any show of famil-iarity. I was sure that this stranger had never once looked at me…even though she always spoke to me and reminded me of painful and distant events… When I saw her at the Government Office, I decided to break up with Ema that very day.

"Madrazo is an extraordinary guy!" I said in Don Ignacio's salon, envying the politician's gesture of freedom and feeling humiliated by my cowardice.

Don Ignacio peered at me warily. The pink-painted walls were all the same, and Ema shifted restlessly, crossing her legs to reveal her black garter.

"Extraordinary, you say?" Don Ignacio laughed derisively.

"No one ever dares to renounce anything…" I declared, feeling faint from panic. My words received no reply. Don Ignacio's family looked at me in silence. It was hard to explain that, for me, the infamous renunciation had become bound up with my ignominious acceptance, and that it mysteriously intruded into my thoughts again and again.

Why didn't I say right then that I admired the politician for executing an act that I myself was incapable of? I took my leave confusedly, and I didn't go back to the house on Calle de Montes Cárpatos for the next two days.

At night my room filled with piano chords, and the reflections in the sky were erased. That night, a friend's recent suicide seemed understandable: he had also refused to accept failure… What failure? I didn't know.

I saw her again in the cafe at the Paris Cinema. I was going to the movies a lot in those days. It was a way to escape Ema and the constant dates with her that had become just as boring as my business meetings. I would duck her kisses, and she didn't seem to care all that much: "I'll have you forever," she said without saying a word. Dazed, I looked at her mouth smeared with red lipstick. Was it true? Things happened in the movies that never happened to me, and that's why I took refuge in the darkened theaters.

When I saw her she was drinking a vanilla milkshake. Her dress was the same color as the ice cream, and it didn't have sleeves, but rather two almost geometrical ruffles that looked like small, stiff wings. I grabbed a table near hers and caught a whiff of her metallic perfume. She didn't look at me. She leaned over and nibbled at the straw, then sipped the cold liquid without a change in her expression. She stood and left the cafe. I caught up with her under the marquee.

"Miss, may I accompany you?"

She looked at the neon shining in the glass marquee.

"Why not?" she said, though I don't know if I heard her voice or imagined it. I led her to my car, and she got in beside me. She never once glanced at me. She was busy looking up through the windshield at the sky. She guided me wordlessly to a dark side street in Coyoacán. As I drove, I looked over at her crossed legs: she wasn't wearing stockings, and her skin shone like silver. She didn't seem cold, and she seemed to take up no space. I parked the car in front of a white house and turned toward the stranger, who didn't react. I took her in my arms, and she felt cold and liquid: it was like embracing a river. Her cool mouth seemed to enter mine, dissolving, making me melt in a brand-new sensation. She opened her eyes and slipped from my arms; I saw her on her feet in the night, and I followed her. Swift as a snake she moved to the front door and pushed it open. She did it all soundlessly, seeming to feel no resistance from objects. I went in behind her and found myself in a small vestibule where a milky white staircase led down to the basement. The young woman took off her shoes and hurried down the stairs. I followed, admiring her mother-of-pearl heels and her nearly liquid ankles. We came to a small door and she opened it soundlessly, then led me into a room where there was a bed made of dark wood and a white animal-skin rug on the floor. The bedspread, pillowcases, curtains, and porcelain were all deeply cold and white. She leaned against the closed door and looked up at the ceiling with her light blue eyes. Then, very slowly, she lowered the winglike straps of her dress and uncovered her bare torso, where her breasts shone like two little piles of snow. I wanted to move closer to her, but I saw that she kept lowering her dress until it fell at her feet. She was left naked, illuminating the room like a shining star and looking with her statue eyes at the very low ceiling of her room. I took a few steps and ran my fingertips along the contours of that mysterious body; without looking at me, she went over to the bed and lay down on the bright white bedspread. "You do not believe in beauty," I perhaps imagined her saying to me, while her naked, elongated body seemed to turn into a luminous river. Through a high window covered in white muslin, the faint light of the stars shone in. The room was underground and the body that lay beside mine was silver. It was not of this world. Being with her was like entering the luminous ore of a secret mine, where hidden treasures reappear in ever more precious shapes. At times I had the feeling that I was not with anyone, though the most unexpected pleasures enveloped me. The body slipped from my arms and reappeared in the same place, ever more brilliant, ever more translucent. I repeated, "I love you, I love you," but the words didn't convey what I felt for her.

"You will not see me tomorrow…right?" she asked.

I foolishly swore that I would see her every minute of every day. She didn't reply but instead straightened up in bed like a beautiful fountain and pointed to the light filtering in through the little window up near the ceiling of her room. Then she jumped out of bed and climbed up onto a stool that was under the window, raised the white curtains, and looked distractedly at the green grass that grew in the yard, which started at the windowpane. We were underground; above, the greens were tender beyond the glass.

"It's six in the morning," she said, breathing in the freshness of the grass.

Something ferocious shoved me from the bed. I got dressed in a hurry and went over to the woman, who looked at me from atop the stool. I embraced her crystalline knees, and left…

"I'll be back tonight," I said, looking at her from the doorway, astonishingly perfect, astonishingly brazen.

I was met by the familiar smells of my house and by the voice of my mother, who was just then eating breakfast. On a chair in her room was a peacock-blue velvet dress. Terrified, I remembered it was my wedding day.

"You rascal…how was your bachelor party?"

From that moment on, the telephone rang nonstop: it was always Ema and Don Ignacio; they wanted to time our departures so we'd arrive at San Jacinto together. The atrium and the naves of the church were stuffed with feathers and satin hangings. The wedding smelled of perfume and incense, and beside me, covered in a thicket of dark veils, Ema looked very satisfied as the priest offered up his threats. "I'll go see her tonight," I repeated over and over, while her naked body moved like liquid between the altars. In the sacristy she came up to me and kissed me on the mouth while everyone was shaking my hand in a sign of mourning. I saw her disappear among the guests like a thin column of quicksilver…

In Acapulco, I've seen absolutely nothing. Ema covers me like a thick layer of earth, unmovable by any miracle. I know I'm not going to get her back; that's my punishment for having renounced beauty… I will never again find that precious ore…for I know now that she was Mercury…

OUR LIVES ARE RIVERS

For Sofía Garro

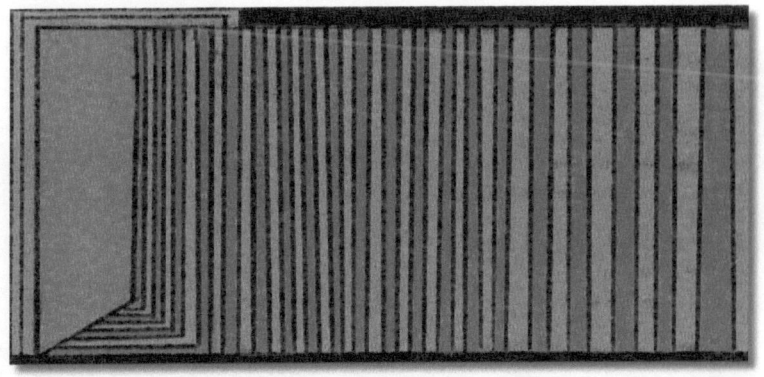

There was the general, much taller than the rest, with his open military doublet revealing his throat, a lock of hair falling between his light-colored eyes. He swung his arms as he walked, and he walked nonchalantly, he walked disinterestedly, and he looked at the others with laughter. He stopped when told to. Indolently, his weight on one leg and a cigarette in his hand, he peered at the world like a cat waking up, and he raised an arm to wave goodbye. The sort of goodbye men give when they're off to take a stroll around the square. Next his knees bent as he fell slowly backward beside his open grave, and then there was only half his body, his eyes narrowed and his throat dripping blood. Now the lieutenant's arm was holding the gun up to the general's temple as he gave him the finishing blow. And finally, the general's head asleep on the earth, a little hole near his temple from which a black trickle flowed into the loose earth.

Beneath the photographs:

GENERAL RUEDA QUIJANO WALKS INSOLENTLY TOWARD THE FIRING WALL.

"GENERAL, WHAT IS YOUR LAST WISH?"

"A CIGARETTE."

THE GENERAL SMOKES WITHOUT DROPPING THE ASH FROM HIS CIGARETTE; THEN, SMILING, HE RAISES HIS HAND AND WAVES: GOODBYE!

A SHARP EXPLOSION ENDS HIS LIFE.

THE LIEUTENANT GIVES THE DEAD MAN A COUP DE GRÂCE.

GENERAL RUEDA QUIJANO WAS TWENTY-SEVEN YEARS OLD AT THE MOMENT OF HIS DEATH.

In those days the girls were unaware that twenty-seven was very young. However, the tall, carefree general who walked reluctantly toward his death tormented them. There he was, waving goodbye, smiling, displaying the beauty of his teeth and the languor of his body when confronting the violent act of dying. The rifles so near his eyes, and behind him a time that the photographers had not recorded with their cameras, a time known only to him. In the books was the head of a moribund Alexander, and in the newspaper was the dirt of some place in Mexico, and on it, the head and throat of the moribund general. He had died early the previous morning, and the girls gazed at his death in the still afternoon of the following day. His steps, his indolence, his beauty, were irrecoverable.

The newspaper lying open on the red tiles of the court-yard gallery was yellowed and dry; its black ink images showed how a twenty-seven-year-old Mexican general died.

The girls examined his riding boots, his gabardine pants, his open doublet, his long strides, the swing of his arms, and his eyes before dying. They also examined the soldiers' serious faces, and then the general's powerful throat and his head lying in the loose earth. They looked at each other. The two of them were stretched out on the ground, facedown, looking at the same death of the same general.

"He's never getting up again," said Eva, pointing to the earth in the newspaper.

"Never."

"Never. Never ever," Eva insisted.

The soldiers and the lieutenant had changed places, and General Rueda Quijano was motionless as a broken statue on the dry earth.

"He said *Goodbye*, in English."

"It's a password," replied Eva.

"A magic word?"

"Yes, so the angels with swords come to get him."

Through the still afternoon, orange legions of armed angels went past. The trees shook their branches, and the house, overcome by the thunder, shrank before the grandeur of their flight until it became a little lost pebble on a great plain. The general's passing into the warriors' world produced this roar of swords and then this silence, this nothing, this broken throat, this never, this dry newspaper, open on the tiles.

"The government killed him. You have to be really careful with the government," Eva explained, opening her eyes very wide and staring at her sister.

"Have you seen him, the government?"

"Yeah… One time I did… Rutilio told me, The goddam government is murderous…"

"He killed General Rueda Quijano."

"He killed him forever." Eva said these words gravely.

"Forever…? But we're reincarnated…"

The circle of reincarnations, like the merry-go-round, started to turn, happy and sad, like the music of "México, febrero 23" in the courtyard of the house. General Rueda Quijano went past on an orange horse adorned with white feathers, his hand raised; "*Goodbye*," he called to them, and disappeared. Then, on the same orange horse, he reappeared. "I'm back," he told them in a cheerful voice, and disappeared a second time. He had been born again.

"But we don't have the same hair, or the same eyes; that's why the government kills forever," Eva said seriously.

"He's never going to get up."

In the newspaper, the general was still spread out on the dry ground. His slightly open mouth would never again say *Goodbye*. His immobile throat was still torn open in the dry sheet of paper, and his hair was motionless inside the frozen ink. The silent soldiers looked at him; no morning, no afternoon, would they hear his voice again, or see him walk. They had killed him forever.

"Never ever," Eva repeated.

She put her face on the newspaper and was still. Leli copied her. The two of them motionless atop the motionless general. The house was as still as they were, as if the government had put it to death. The afternoon was made of newspaper, just as the morning had been of photographs. The sound of some footsteps crinkling the dry paper of the afternoon drew closer to them, but their faces did not move away from the executed general.

"Leli, girl, your uncle is inviting you to dinner."

It was Ceferino, their uncle Boni's servant. Leli looked at the general walking disdainfully toward his death.

"Come, child, your uncle is very sad," Ceferino insisted.

Since Hebe's death, their uncle was always sad. He lived alone, pacing the courtyard gallery of his house, refusing to see anyone, even his brother. The only person he talked to was Leli, and that's why she could not refuse his invitation. Leli thought she could see Hebe rocking on the sofa, her blonde hair lit up by the afternoon sun as she repeated, "I want to leave this place." And one day she left. Where did she go? Who knows! There were so many places to go after death, it was hard to tell which of them Hebe and General Rueda Quijano might have gone to.

"Child, I'm waiting for you."

Leli lifted her face from the newspaper and took a last look at the general walking with long strides toward the firing wall. She got up, smiled, and started taking her own long strides, swinging her arms indolently like the general.

"*Goodbye!*" she said to her sister in a disdainful voice, and went out to the street with Ceferino behind her.

"The government is really murderous."

"Yes, the government will execute any man in Mexico," Ceferino replied, walking beside her through the hushed vestibules.

"I'm a Mexican man too," said Leli, who just then was walking like the Mexican general, through a landscape of the executed, with long strides, indifferent to the sadness of losing his life.

Ceferino looked at her mockingly.

"A Mexican man...? You're a little girl, and so blonde. You're Spanish."

Ceferino's words hurt her: he didn't want her to be a Mexican man. She stayed silent and breathed the afternoon rising up into the sky. In the distance, the orange-and-violet hills had fallen still, no iguanas, no hawks, no wind. The river ran without water, dry like the newspaper spread out in the courtyard of her house. The dry stones of the street were strewn with peanut shells. The balconies were closed and the silent kiosk in the plaza was like a funerary monument. The most important thing in this life was that we died. All the people who went to market died, and all the ones who lived inside the houses. The women who fed swans in Sydney died, too. She had seen their picture in the Sunday paper; they wore little white hats and smiled in spite of their sad luck. There were days like that one, when death's skinny fingers touched the streets and the trees, to make us feel that nothing contained in this whole world was ours. At her uncle's house, she found the same grief left by Hebe's death, the same leafy trees, the same dogs sprawled in the courtyard, the same deer running in the garden, and the same scent of Camel cigarettes. Everything was the same, momentary and fleeting, and that's why she didn't understand why Ceferino wouldn't want her to be Mexican.

"Uncle, why are we Spanish?"

"Because we speak with the Z."

One letter, and it kept her from being General Rueda Quijano. Ceferino, sitting on the windowsill, smiled in satisfaction. On the little table in the courtyard, beside the cigarettes and the ashtray, was the newspaper with the executed general.

"He was only twenty-seven," her uncle said, looking at the image of the fallen general and shaking his head incredulously.

Ceferino rolled a cigarette and turned to gaze at the purple outlines of the plants. Leli, sitting on a tall chair, was engrossed in looking at her feet in their huaraches as they swung in the air. Her toes were pink and small like carnations before they opened, but one day they would no longer be pink and no one would see them anymore, not even Leli herself. They would lie there like the executed general's feet in the irrevocable silence of the newspaper. Her uncle and Ceferino were silent; they, too, were thinking about the disappearance of their fingers and toes. The whole house was silent, discerning its own death. After a little while Fili came in, walking barefoot and carrying the tray with hibiscus water, Bols gin, and lemons. She said hello and left without making a sound. That night, Leli and her uncle would dine alone at the giant table with its starched tablecloth, and Fili would serve figs, nuts, and custard.

"Uncle, how old are you?"

"Thirty-one."

The number told her nothing; she looked at him to see

what a thirty-one-year-old man was like: he had blond hair and a white silk shirt; he smelled as always of aftershave, and his yellow eyes were sad.

"What did your uncle say to you?" they would ask her at home.

"He read to me: *Life Is a Dream.*"

"Boni is going to commit suicide," her father would reply, looking at her with the same yellow eyes as her uncle. He, too, always wore a white shirt, and sometimes he would say, very frightened, "God has forsaken us."

Her uncle moved closer to the newspaper and looked at General Rueda Quijano for a long time.

"He wanted to die."

He poured a little Bols gin into a glass, mixed it with water and added some drops of lemon, took a sip, and walked thoughtfully down the courtyard gallery. He walked it many times up and down, down and up, and then he went over to Leli.

"Do you want to die?"

She reflected for a long time before answering. What did it mean to die?

"If it's daytime in death, then yes, I want to," she replied.

Her uncle lifted a blonde lock and caressed her forehead.

"It's always daytime in death. That's why I want to die, but death has me pacing around this house…"

"We all die, sir—why rush it?" Ceferino asked in a slow voice.

But Uncle Boni was impatient, and he drummed his

fingers on the newspaper.

"That's how one should die, at the height of beauty," he said, pointing to General Rueda Quijano.

There was no consolation: there they sat, waiting for night to fall and death to come. And then? Then she had no answer; the dogs didn't have it either, and they lay motionless, waiting as well. Some deer came up to Leli; tamely, they ate the cigarettes she held out to them. Leli looked at Ceferino's unmoving profile and at her uncle's incessant pacing in the desolate courtyard, and she felt that she would always be like this: looking at anguish, Camel cigarettes in her open hand, offering them to deer with brooding noses.

"The general lost patience," said Ceferino.

Leli understood General Rueda Quijano's impatience. She would do the same: she would go straight ahead to break her days, walking toward the firing wall, swinging her arms, smiling disdainfully to get ahead of the day, and then she would say to "the others" *Goodbye*, and she would suddenly open up to the Always Daytime of death, where the orange angels with shining espadas blades lived.

"When I grow up, I'm going to be a Mexican general."

Ceferino turned to look at her in displeasure, but he didn't feel like replying, and after a few seconds he turned back toward the trees.

"You'll be just as handsome as General Rueda Quijano," said her uncle approvingly.

"He told them *Goodbye*; he told them they were traitors," said Ceferino, looking at the deer that were peering out from behind the trees.

"Told who?" she asked.

"The government."

The three of them were again as quiet as the dead general in the newspaper. The afternoon sank down behind the garden walls. Boni's steps kept turning in the shadows. A perfumed smoke followed the comings and goings of his white shirt. It was useless for him to turn; Hebe was in the center of the circle, and he remained fixed and spellbound, like the general inside the newspaper. The whole house was inside that day, in the month of April, in which Hebe had stopped rocking on the sofa, had stopped spreading out her blonde hair to illuminate the sun. The weeks and holidays solidified into that immobile April day; the heat of the watered gardenias hovering over the ground and the unbreathable air of the closed-off rooms turned permanent.

Boni's voice emerged, like a magic incantation from a corner of the courtyard:

> *Our lives are fated as the rivers*
> *that gather downward to the sea*
> *we know as Death…*

Manrique's words, recited aloud, dissolved the stillness that immobilized the house, and the night suddenly began to sail down a broad, rushing waterway. The melancholic voice that uttered them also entered a river that twisted and turned through a sad landscape, and little by little, everything started to gently rock along: Ceferino, sitting on the windowsill facing the courtyard, floated in the yellow current of his river, slowly moving toward a luminous sea. The chair

Leli was sitting on entered a cold current, and she also went sailing along, her hands outstretched to feed cigarettes to the deer that floated alongside her, two neighboring streams that in turn ran toward the sea. It was easy to live sliding soundlessly toward death. A soft wind caressed their hair, and the landscape passed sweetly before their eyes, unreachable in its untouched beauty. Boni's voice sketched salons and remote celebrations, the dampness of the mountains and trees stirring with birds. Then, when Boni had fallen silent, time kept flowing from a secret spring and the skies and the patios of the houses kept on sliding like the moons through the clouds. They went to the table, and Fili and María came in holding their trays high, so the water of their rivers wouldn't splash the nuts and custards. Their black braids flew lightly across their backs and their purple petticoats floated like flags planted in two rivers. The whole night advanced inside a river that carried stars, mouths, branches, winds, and executed Mexican generals.

Leli ate the custard knowing that a wet breeze bathed her hair, and that she, sitting at the head of the starched table, was advancing toward a blue sea bathed in yellow suns.

"Uncle, do the rivers of generals have rapids?"

The image spread in the violence of the newspaper suddenly interrupted the race toward the sea. The loss of the general's beauty was irreparable, and his broken forehead was useless. His bent legs carried him weakly backward as though in spite of himself, toward some unknown place. Leli had the impression that he went alone, and that he didn't want to reach that strange place into which the soldiers' bullets were violently hurling him. The custard turned absurd in the white china. It was no longer tempting. She lay the spoon in the dish and waited for a reply from her uncle, who was looking at her with his yellow eyes full of sorrow.

"Yes, they have rapids; that's why they only last twenty-seven years."

"What about your river?"

Her uncle averted his eyes and stared at a point as distant as the one the general had been looking at before he received the final bullet.

"Mine...? Mine has many curves..."

"What about Ceferino's?"

"It's very long and crosses many valleys..."

Leli thought that Ceferino's river must be very old and have seen many rains, many suns, and many heartaches. How long had Ceferino been advancing in his huaraches, with his white hat over his black eyes and his pink shirt wet with the water of his river? Who knows! No one could tell her, not even Ceferino, because surely he had forgotten the landscapes he had sailed through over the course of so many years. She folded her hands on the tablecloth, resolved her eyes, and asked her question bravely.

"What about mine?"

Boni sat for a long time examining her serious expression, her still hands, and her brave eyes.

"Yours has rapids. It's the river of a Mexican general... But all of the rivers, yours, mine, Ceferino's, and General Rueda Quijano's, lead to the same sea."

His yellow eyes met the girl's and his lips offered her a smile. The grief of the newspaper dissolved in his words, and Leli knew that there in the sea they were all the same, and that General Rueda Quijano would never again be alone, walking disdainfully toward the firing wall, watched by the soldiers' serious eyes and the absurd cameras of the press photographers. The place where the Mauser bullets had taken him was the same place where her own river of violent rapids would lead: a blue sea of yellow suns. From within that radiance, the general watched her approach.

ELENA GARRO (1916–1998) was a novelist, playwright, short-story writer, journalist, and the inventor of magical realism, though she rejected the term as "a cheap marketing label." The author of over 40 books, she wrote about the violence embedded in everyday life, with a focus on children, women, and indigenous people.

MEGAN MCDOWELL has translated many of the most important Latin American writers working today. Her translations have won numerous prizes, including the National Book Award, and have been nominated for the International Booker Prize four times. She is from Richmond, Kentucky, and lives in Barcelona, Spain.

ÁLVARO ENRIGUE is a Mexican writer whose most recent novel is *You Dreamed of Empires*. His books have been awarded the Herralde Prize, the Barcelona Prize, and the Poniatowska Prize. He teaches Latin American Literature at Hofstra University and lives with his family in New York City.